Riding with Shadows

Sienna Steel

Contents

Chapter 1

The roar of engines and the scent of leather and gasoline filled the air, mingling with the laughter and chatter of the crowd. I stood on the outskirts of the biker rally, my heart racing with a mixture of excitement and nervousness. I'd always admired the rebellious freedom of bikers from afar, but today was different-I was actually here, soaking in the chaos and thrill.

As I wandered past rows of gleaming motorcycles, one bike in particular caught my eye. Its sleek black frame and chrome details were stunning, but it was the rider that really drew my attention. He was a vision of confidence, maneuvering his bike with a skill that seemed almost effortless. The crowd cheered, and I found myself cheering too, though my voice was barely audible over the roar of engines.

It was then that he spotted me. His gaze locked onto mine as he revved his engine, a playful grin spreading across his face. I felt a rush of heat as he made his way over, the crowd parting like waves before him.

"Hey there," he said, his voice carrying effortlessly above the noise. "I haven't seen you around here before."

I laughed, feeling a bit self-conscious. "Guilty as charged. I'm more of a spectator than a rider."

He raised an eyebrow, clearly intrigued. "Well, that's a shame. Spectating is only half the fun. Ever thought about giving riding a try?"

I was taken aback. "Me? Ride a bike? I wouldn't even know where to start."

He extended a hand, the gesture warm and inviting. "I'm Jake. How about I teach you? It'll be a lot more fun than just watching."

I hesitated for a moment, my mind racing with a mix of fear and excitement. Finally, I took his hand, feeling a jolt of electricity at the touch. "Okay, Jake. Let's do it."

Jake led me to a bike parked nearby, its chrome gleaming under the sun. He handed me a helmet with a grin. "First rule of riding: always look cool, even if you're scared out of your mind."

I chuckled nervously as I put on the helmet, trying to mask my anxiety. "Got it. Looking cool while trembling in fear."

Jake climbed onto the bike and motioned for me to join him. "You'll be riding behind me today. I'll show you the ropes."

As we started moving, I clung to him, my heart pounding in my chest. The wind rushed against my face, making me feel both exhilarated and terrified. Jake's easy laughter was a comforting presence.

"You're doing great," he shouted over the noise, though I could barely hear him. "Just remember to lean with the bike."

I tried to follow his instructions, though my body felt stiff and awkward. Jake's playful teasing continued, his voice full of encouragement. "If you can manage to keep your balance, you might just survive the day."

I shot him a mock glare. "Survival is overrated. I'm here for the experience."

The laughter in his voice was contagious. "Good attitude. We might actually make a biker out of you yet."

As the ride continued, I gradually loosened up, beginning to enjoy the thrill of it all. Jake's confidence was infectious, and his teasing made me laugh despite my nerves. By the time we returned to the rally, I was grinning from ear to ear, a newfound sense of adventure coursing through me.

We dismounted, and Jake gave me a friendly pat on the back. "Not bad for a first timer. How about we make this a regular thing?"

I looked up at him, my heart racing for a different reason now. "I'd like that. A lot."

He smiled, his eyes sparkling with mischief. "Great. It's a date. Or, well, a ride. Same thing, really."

We parted ways for the evening, but as I walked away, I couldn't shake the feeling that this was the start of something extraordinary. The thrill of the ride, the laughter, and the way Jake made me feel-everything was a whirlwind, but it was exactly what I needed.

Chapter 2

Jake and I spent nearly every weekend at the biker park. Each lesson felt like a new adventure, and somehow, between the revving engines and winding roads, we were getting to know each other on a deeper level.

One Saturday morning, Jake showed up with an extra spark in his eye. "Ready for today's challenge?" he asked, a teasing grin on his face.

I raised an eyebrow. "What's the challenge this time?"

He gestured to the bike, already warmed up and waiting. "Today's the day you go solo. Time to see what you've learned."

I felt a mix of excitement and nerves twist in my stomach. "Solo? Like, alone?"

Jake's grin widened. "Yep. I'll be right behind you, but it's your turn to take control."

I took a deep breath and climbed onto the bike, my hands trembling slightly as I adjusted my gloves. "Okay, Jake. I'm ready. I think."

Jake gave me a thumbs-up. "Just remember to keep it smooth. Lean into the turns and breathe."

I nodded, focusing on the task at hand. I twisted the throttle gently, and the bike surged forward. My heart raced as I navigated the first turn. Jake's voice was a comforting presence behind me, cheering me on.

"Nice and steady!" he called out. "You're doing great!"

I managed a few wobbly turns but quickly found my rhythm. Each successful maneuver made me feel more confident. Jake's encouragement was a steady boost, and I found myself smiling, despite the nerves.

After a few laps around the park, I finally came to a smooth stop, feeling like I had just conquered the world. Jake was there in a flash, his face beaming with pride.

"That was fantastic!" he exclaimed, clapping me on the back. "You nailed it."

I couldn't help but grin, feeling a rush of accomplishment. "Thanks, Jake. I couldn't have done it without your help."

He chuckled, removing his helmet. "If you keep riding like that, I might need to start taking lessons from you."

We walked back to the parking area, the sunlight casting long shadows across the pavement. As we sat on the curb, Jake and I shared stories and dreams about what lay ahead.

"I always wanted to ride across the country," Jake said, looking out at the horizon with a thoughtful expression. "There's something about seeing new places, meeting new people."

I nodded, feeling inspired. "That sounds amazing. I've always dreamed of exploring more, too. Maybe one day, we could do that together."

Jake's eyes sparkled with mischief. "You mean you're planning on sticking around for more adventures?"

I laughed, nudging him playfully. "Well, if you keep making it this much fun, I might just have to."

Jake smirked. "Guess I'll have to keep up the good work then. Maybe you'll be my official riding partner."

I looked at him, my heart fluttering. "I'd like that. A lot."

As we chatted, the conversation flowed effortlessly. Jake's humor and kindness made every moment feel special. It wasn't just about riding anymore; it was about us building something meaningful together.

Jake leaned closer, his voice dropping to a playful whisper. "So, when's your first big solo ride? Planning on taking me on a cross-country trip anytime soon?"

I rolled my eyes, grinning. "Slow down, speed racer. Let's start with mastering the park, and we'll see where it goes from there."

Jake chuckled, wrapping an arm around me. "Deal. But I'm holding you to that cross-country ride eventually."

As we wrapped up for the day, I felt a warm glow inside. The road ahead was full of possibilities, and with Jake by my side, I was eager to see where our journey would take us.

Chapter 3

One weekend, Jake and I decided to break away from the usual park routine and explore some scenic routes. The plan was simple: hit the open road and let the wind guide us. Little did I know, this would turn into one of the best days ever.

We set off early in the morning, the sun still low in the sky. Jake led the way, his bike slicing through the air with effortless grace. I followed behind, my heart soaring with each mile. The countryside stretched out before us, lush and green, with wildflowers dotting the landscape. I couldn't help but marvel at the beauty around me.

Jake glanced back occasionally, a playful smirk on his face. "How's it feel out there? Are you keeping up?"

I laughed, feeling a bit winded but thrilled. "Keeping up? I'm trying not to crash into every tree I see!"

He chuckled, his voice carrying over the roar of our engines. "Don't worry, I've got an eye on you. Just remember, if you can't avoid the trees, at least try not to make it a habit."

I shot him a mock glare, though I couldn't help but smile. "I'll do my best. No promises about avoiding every bump, though."

Our ride took us down winding roads and through charming little towns. We stopped occasionally to stretch our legs and grab snacks from quirky roadside stands. At one of these stops, I tried to do a little trick Jake had taught me-rev the bike while standing still.

Let's just say it didn't go as planned. I ended up doing an awkward dance, trying to balance while the bike wobbled beneath me. Jake watched from a safe distance, shaking with laughter.

"Having some trouble there?" he called out, barely containing his amusement.

I stuck out my tongue at him, though I was grinning. "Hey, it's a work in progress. I'm sure I'll have it down by the time we're old and gray."

Jake walked over and steadied the bike, his eyes twinkling with affection. "Well, if you need any more practice, you know where to find me."

As the day wore on, we continued our ride, each mile bringing us closer. Our conversations ranged from silly to serious, and I found myself opening up in ways I hadn't expected. We talked about our favorite childhood memories, our biggest fears, and our wildest dreams.

I felt a flutter in my chest, a warmth that was more than just the sun on my face. We were riding together, sharing dreams and moments, and it felt right.

We stopped for a break at a picturesque overlook, the sun setting in a blaze of oranges and pinks. Jake and I sat on the grass, our bikes parked nearby. The view was breathtaking, but it was the company that made it perfect.

"So, what's your biggest fear?" Jake asked, his tone more serious now.

I looked out at the horizon, thinking. "I guess it's not living life to the fullest. Settling for something less than what I'm capable of."

Jake's expression was thoughtful. "I get that. For me, it's not finding someone who understands me. Someone who gets what riding means to me."

I turned to him, my heart pounding. "Well, I think you've found that person."

He smiled, his eyes meeting mine with a look that made my pulse race. "I think so too."

The silence between us was comfortable, filled with an unspoken understanding. As the sun dipped below the horizon, Jake leaned in closer, his hand still holding mine.

"I really like you, Emily," he said softly, his voice full of sincerity. "This-everything we're doing-it feels right. I hope you feel the same way."

I looked into his eyes, feeling a surge of emotion. "I do. I really do."

Our lips met in a gentle kiss, the world around us fading away. It was a moment of pure connection, a blending of our dreams and our feelings. As we pulled away, Jake's smile was radiant.

Chapter 4

Jake's POV:

Today was one of those days that felt like it was plucked straight out of a dream. Emily and I had planned a ride to one of my favorite spots-a secluded overlook with a stunning view. It had become our little tradition, a day spent together away from the chaos of everyday life.

I waited for her at the bike park, my excitement barely contained. When she finally arrived, wearing that familiar, radiant smile, it felt like the day was already perfect.

"Ready for our adventure?" I asked, as I helped her with her helmet.

She grinned, her eyes sparkling with excitement. "Definitely. I've been looking forward to this all week."

We hit the road, the wind whipping through our hair and the sun shining brightly. Emily rode close behind me, and I couldn't help but steal glances at her through the mirrors. Seeing her enjoying herself so much, looking like she belonged on the bike, made me feel incredibly proud.

The ride was smooth and exhilarating. We talked and laughed over the roar of the engines, sharing stories and making plans for the future. I loved how easily we fell into conversation, how our dreams and aspirations seemed to intertwine with each mile we covered.

As we neared our destination, I could see the anticipation in Emily's eyes. We pulled up to the overlook, and I watched her take in the view-a sweeping panorama of rolling hills and distant mountains. It was breathtaking, but seeing her reaction made it even more special.

"Wow," she said, her voice filled with awe. "This is incredible."

I grinned, feeling a deep sense of satisfaction. "I'm glad you like it. I've been coming here for years, and it's always been my favorite spot."

We set up our picnic near the edge, the soft blanket contrasting with the rough ground beneath. As we unpacked our lunch, I couldn't help but admire how perfectly we fit together-both as partners on the bike and as companions in life.

"So, what's next for us?" Emily asked, her tone more serious than usual as we sat down.

I looked at her, my heart full. "You know, I've been thinking a lot about our future. About how much I want us to share these moments forever."

Emily smiled softly, her eyes reflecting the sunlight. "I'd like that too. A lot."

I reached over and took her hand, feeling the warmth of her touch. "I want to promise you something. I'll always ride safely, no matter what. I know how much it means to you, and it means just as much to me."

Her gaze softened, and she squeezed my hand. "Thank you, Jake. That means more to me than you know."

I looked into her eyes, my emotions raw and sincere. "Emily, you've become so important to me. I never thought I'd find someone who makes me feel this way-someone who under-stands me, who makes every ride and every moment better just by being there."

She leaned in, her voice barely a whisper. "I feel the same way. I rely on you, Jake. You're more than just a ride; you're everything."

I pulled her into a gentle embrace, feeling a surge of affection and gratitude. As we held each other, I knew that this was where I wanted to be. The future was still full of uncertainty, but with Emily by my side, it felt like we could handle anything.

We spent the rest of the afternoon talking about our dreams, our plans, and the life we wanted to build together. It was a perfect day-one of those rare moments where every-thing just seemed right.

As the sun began to set, casting a warm glow over the landscape, I took a deep breath, feeling content and hopeful. With Emily, every day was an adventure, and I couldn't wait to see where our journey would take us next.

Chapter 5

Emily's POV:

It was a beautiful Saturday morning when Jake and I set out for our usual ride. The sun was shining, the roads were clear, and we were both in high spirits. We planned to hit up a new route we'd heard about-a scenic drive that promised amazing views and a bit of adventure.

Everything seemed perfect until Jake's mood shifted slightly. As we cruised along, he glanced in the rearview mirror, his brow furrowing.

"Hey, Em," he said, his voice slightly tense, "I need to mention something."

I looked over, noticing the change in his demeanor. "What's up?"

"There's been this truck following us," he said, trying to sound casual but not quite succeeding. "I've seen it a few times now, and it's starting to get a little weird."

I frowned, glancing around as we rode. "A truck? What's so odd about that?"

Jake shrugged, though I could tell he was trying to down-play his concern. "It's not just the truck itself. It's been showing up on some of our routes, like it's intentionally following us. And it's been driving a bit too close for comfort."

My stomach twisted with unease. "Are you sure it's the same truck? Maybe it's just a coincidence."

Jake nodded, his grip on the handlebars tightening slightly. "Yeah, I'm sure. It's got a big dent on the side and a faded paint job. I've seen it a few times now, always at a distance, but it's getting more frequent."

We continued riding, but I couldn't shake the feeling of unease. Every time I glanced in the mirror, I half-expected to see that truck lurking behind us. The roads were open and empty, which made the possibility of being followed even more unsettling.

As we took a break at a small roadside café, I watched Jake scan the area, his expression guarded. He seemed more on edge than usual, and it was affecting me too. I tried to stay calm, but the thought of someone-or something-watching us from the shadows was disconcerting.

"So, what do you think we should do?" I asked, trying to keep my voice steady.

Jake looked at me, his eyes serious. "For now, let's just be aware. If it gets worse, we might need to do something more. Maybe change up our routes or, if it really gets bad, involve the authorities."

I nodded, trying to push away the creeping worry. "Alright. I trust you. Just keep me in the loop, okay?"

He gave me a reassuring smile, though it didn't quite reach his eyes. "Definitely. I don't want you to be worried. We'll handle it."

We finished our break and headed back out on the road. The truck didn't appear during our ride back, but the unease lingered. Jake's usual carefree demeanor was replaced with a focused vigilance, and I could tell he was more concerned than he let on.

As we rode side by side, I could see the tension in his posture, and it made my heart ache. I wanted to believe that it was just a coincidence, but the fact that Jake was so worried made me anxious too. We were supposed to be enjoying our time together, not looking over our shoulders.

When we finally arrived back at the park, Jake gave me a reassuring squeeze on the shoulder. "We'll be okay. Let's just keep an eye out and stay smart."

I smiled, though it was tinged with worry. "Okay. I'm with you."

As we parted ways for the evening, the sight of that mysterious truck kept replaying in my mind. It was like a dark cloud hanging over what should have been a perfect day. I knew Jake would keep me safe, but the feeling of being watched made everything seem a little less secure.

I couldn't shake the feeling that things were about to change, and not for the better. The road ahead seemed a bit darker now, and I hoped that whatever was trailing us would stay out of our way.

Chapter 6

Emily's POV:

It was supposed to be just another ride, another day in our endless adventure. But that morning, everything felt off. The sky was overcast, casting a gray pallor over the roads. Jake and I had planned a quick trip to grab coffee and hit our favorite scenic route. It was supposed to be lighthearted and simple, like so many rides before.

As we headed out, the truck reappeared. My heart sank when I saw it-same faded paint job, same dent on the side. It was tailing us again, just like Jake had mentioned. My anxiety spiked, and I could see Jake's concern in the way he kept glancing in the mirrors.

"Jake," I said, my voice trembling slightly, "the truck is back."

He nodded, his face set in a determined expression. "I see it. Let's stay calm and keep our distance. We'll be fine."

But the truck didn't just follow us. It started to close the gap, its engine roaring menacingly. I could feel the tension in the air, a heavy, oppressive weight that made my heart pound. Jake kept his cool, maneuvering the bike with precision, but the truck's aggressive approach made it clear it wasn't just a coincidence anymore.

"Jake, it's getting closer!" I shouted, trying to keep my voice steady.

He tightened his grip on the handlebars. "Hold on. I'm going to try and lose it."

He accelerated, weaving through the traffic, but the truck was relentless. It was as if it had one goal-us. I could see the determination in Jake's eyes, but there was also a flicker of something else-fear.

In a horrifying instant, the truck rammed into us. I felt the jolt, the violent impact that sent us skidding across the asphalt. My world erupted into chaos-screeching metal, shattering glass, and the blinding pain. Everything happened in a blur, and then there was just darkness.

When I came to, I was lying on the road, my body aching all over. I looked around, disoriented, and saw the truck stopped nearby. People were gathering, shouting, and I could barely process what was happening.

I saw Jake a few feet away, crumpled and motionless. My heart stopped. I tried to move, but pain and shock held me back. I screamed his name, tears streaming down my face. "Jake! No, Jake, please!"

The police arrived quickly, and paramedics started to work on Jake, but I could see the truth in their faces before they even said anything. I was overwhelmed by a numbness, a profound ache that consumed every part of me.

The police arrested the truck driver, a grim-faced man who didn't seem to care about the devastation he'd caused. He was led away in handcuffs, but my mind was too foggy to process any details. All I could focus on was Jake, my love, my partner. I couldn't let go of his hand, even though I knew it was too late.

In my mind, I replayed every happy moment we'd shared-his infectious laugh, the way he looked at me with those warm, adoring eyes, the countless rides that had brought us so close. I thought about our dreams, the future we had planned. It all felt like a cruel joke, taken from me in an instant.

Jake's POV:

As the world slipped away, I could see Emily's face, twisted with agony and shock. I wanted to reach out, to tell her I loved her, to assure her that everything would be okay, but the darkness was closing in. I wished I could hold her one last time, tell her how much she meant to me, how she had changed my life. I had always imagined a future with her, a lifetime of adventures and shared dreams. Now, all I could do was watch helplessly as she struggled with the pain of losing me.

I wanted to tell her how proud I was of her, how much I loved her, and how sorry I was that I couldn't be there to protect her. Every moment of our time together had been a gift, and I would have given anything to have one more day with her.

Emily's POV:

The funeral was a blur of black suits and somber faces. Jake's family was devastated, their grief palpable. I stood among his biker friends, all of us united in our sorrow. They shared stories about Jake, tales of his kindness and his spirit, but it did little to ease the crushing weight of loss.

I clung to Jake's mother, whose tears mirrored my own. We were both grieving for the same man, the same incredible person who had touched our lives in profound ways. His friends spoke of his passion for riding, his love for life, and it was clear that his absence would leave a void that could never be filled.

As I looked at the casket, the reality of Jake's death hit me with a force that nearly knocked me off my feet. He was gone, and all that was left were memories and a deep, unending ache in my heart. I tried to hold onto the moments we shared, the love we had, but the pain of losing him was overwhelming.

The service ended, and as we stood by the gravesite, I felt a cold wind whip through, a reminder of the harsh reality of life. I closed my eyes and whispered a final goodbye to Jake, hoping that wherever he was, he knew how much he was loved and missed.

I would carry his memory with me, through every ride and every adventure, always cherishing the time we had together. The road ahead seemed impossibly dark without him.

Chapter 7

The days after Jake's death felt like they stretched into infinity. Time moved in a haze, each minute a painful reminder of the gaping hole left in my life. The world kept turning, but for me, everything had come to a standstill. The apartment we'd shared now felt empty and alien, every corner a reminder of what we had lost.

The bike sat in the garage, silent and still, a cruel echo of the rides we'd once enjoyed together. I hadn't touched it since that fateful day. The mere thought of mounting it again felt like a betrayal-a violation of the promise I'd made to myself and to Jake.

spent hours sitting in the living room, staring blankly at the walls, my thoughts constantly drifting back to Jake. His laughter, his touch, the way his eyes sparkled when he talked about our future-these memories were both a comfort and a torment. I wanted so desperately to feel his presence, but every moment without him felt like a punishment.

Friends and family reached out, their sympathy wrapped in concern. I was overwhelmed by their kindness but also by their inability to understand the depth of my sorrow. They saw me as a grieving partner, but to me, it felt like I was living in a nightmare where every day was a new level of pain.

Emily, you need to talk to someone," my best friend, Sophie, said one evening as she sat beside me on the couch. Her eyes were red from crying, and I could see the worry etched into her face. "You can't keep this in. It's not good for you."

I looked at her, my heart heavy. "I don't know what to say, Sophie. How do you explain this kind of pain? How do you move on from something like this?"

She took my hand, squeezing it gently. "You don't have to explain anything. Just let us help. We're here for you."

Despite her words, I felt utterly alone. The idea of opening up felt like an impossible task. I was trapped in a world where Jake's absence was a constant, oppressive force. Everything reminded me of him-our favorite restaurants, the places we used to visit, even the little things like the scent of his cologne on a stray shirt.

Jake's family was equally heartbroken, and their grief mirrored mine in many ways. We tried to find solace in each other, but the shared pain only deepened the sense of loss. His mother often called, her voice breaking as she spoke of Jake. "He was such a wonderful person," she'd say, and every word felt like a knife in my chest. I wanted to tell her that I knew, that I had loved him too, but the words never seemed enough.

One afternoon, as I sat in the living room with Jake's old motorcycle jacket draped over my lap, his brother, Mark, stopped by. He was a tall man with a serious demeanor, but today his eyes were soft, filled with a sadness that spoke volumes.

Emily," he said quietly, sitting down next to me, "we're all worried about you. You've been shutting everyone out. We want to be here for you, but you need to let us in."

I looked at him, the weight of his words sinking in. "I don't know how to let anyone in right now. Everything feels so raw. Every time I think I'm starting to heal, something reminds me that Jake is gone, and it all comes crashing down again."

Mark nodded, understanding. "It's okay to feel like this. You don't have to be strong all the time. Grieving is a process, and it takes time."

But time felt like a cruel joke. Each day was a relentless reminder that Jake was never coming back. The future I had envisioned with him was shattered, and I was left to pick up the pieces. I couldn't bear the thought of riding without him, of continuing something that had once been our shared passion. The bike, once a symbol of freedom and joy, had become a symbol of my grief and loss.

Months passed, and the world around me began to adjust to its new normal, but I remained stuck in a cycle of heartache. I'd lost my purpose, and with it, my will to ride. Jake had been my reason to live each day fully, and without him, the joy of riding felt meaningless.

One evening, I found myself sitting on the porch, looking out at the street. The bike was still in the garage, untouched, a reminder of everything I had lost. I made the decision then, a decision that felt both heavy and freeing: I would stop riding. It wasn't just about the bike; it was about honoring Jake's memory in the way I felt was right.

As I looked out at the empty road, I felt a pang of regret mixed with relief. Regret that I couldn't share this passion with him anymore, but relief that I could finally let go of something that had become a painful reminder of his absence. I knew that Jake would have wanted me to move forward, but the idea of moving on felt like a betrayal to everything we had shared.

The days continued to blend together, and though the pain of losing Jake would never truly go away, I slowly began to find small moments of peace. I surrounded myself with the people who cared about me, allowing their support to gradually seep into my fractured heart. They didn't replace Jake, but their presence was a balm for my wounded soul.

Chapter 8

The days turned into weeks, and I found myself drifting further into a void that seemed to swallow everything I once held dear. The bike, which had once been a symbol of joy and freedom, now felt like an anchor dragging me deeper into despair. I was no longer the person I used to be-no longer the woman who reveled in the thrill of the open road with Jake. Instead, I was becoming something else entirely.

The first time I took the bike out without the license plate, I was trembling. The decision felt wrong, like I was crossing a line I could never uncross. But I had reached a point where the idea of riding safely seemed meaningless. Without Jake, the thrill of following the rules felt hollow.

I pulled the plate off the back of the bike, my hands shaking as I unscrewed it. I stuffed it into a drawer, burying it beneath a pile of old maps and greasy rags. With the plate gone, I felt a strange sense of liberation. The bike was no longer just a machine; it was a vehicle for my defiance, a way to embrace the chaos and the darkness.

A week later, the thrill of the underground races was irresistible.

The streets were alive with adrenaline and the roar of engines. I blended into the crowd, my black leather jacket and helmet making me anonymous. I was no longer Emily the grieving fiancée; I was a ghost on the road, a nameless rider chasing the rush of illegal races.

"Hey, you're up next!" a grizzled guy in a leather vest shouted over the din, gesturing toward the starting line. I nodded, my heart racing as I took my place among the other riders.

The signal dropped, and I launched forward, the bike's power surging beneath me. The streets blurred into a streak of lights and shadows, each corner a challenge, each straightaway a chance to push the limits. The thrill of speed and the anonymity of not being recognized made me feel alive in a way I hadn't felt since Jake's death.

One night, as I skidded to a stop after a race, I caught my reflection in the store window nearby.

I barely recognized the woman staring back at me-a ghost of her former self, with a fierce, wild look in her eyes. I was angry and numb, and the racing was my way of screaming into the void, of proving that I could still feel something, anything, beyond the crushing grief.

The more I rode recklessly, the more I questioned if I wanted to keep doing this. Every time I pushed the bike to its limits, part of me wondered if I was throwing away the very essence of what Jake and I had shared. But the other part of me-the part that had lost everything-felt like it had nothing left to lose.

My parents had abandoned me when I was born, and I had no siblings. Jake had been my everything-my partner, my future. And now, with him gone, I felt utterly alone, like there was no one left to care if I threw myself into this reckless existence. The bike was no longer just a way to remember Jake; it had become a way to defy the pain and the emptiness that filled my days.

I began to embrace the darkness, to let it consume me. The illegal races became a daily ritual, a way to escape from the constant ache of my heart. I reveled in the anonymity of it all, the freedom to be whoever I wanted without the weight of my past.

One evening, as I sat on the bike, the roar of the engine beneath me felt like the only thing that could drown out the pain. I looked up at the night sky, the stars distant and indifferent. I was a ghost, lost and drifting, and I had never felt more alive.

In that moment, I accepted that my life had changed ir-revocably. I had embraced the darkness, and though it was terrifying, it was also oddly comforting. I had nothing left to lose, and maybe, just maybe, that was the freedom I had been searching for all along.

Chapter 9

It didn't take long for "Ghost" to become a local legend. Word spread quickly about the anonymous rider who was dominating the underground racing scene and evading law enforcement with unprecedented skill. My reckless escapades had turned me into an enigma-a rider who appeared and vanished like a wisp of smoke, leaving nothing but the roar of the engine and a trail of awe.

The thrill of racing without a license plate was intoxicating. I would hit the streets at night, weaving through traffic and taking tight corners with a speed that left other riders in the dust. I'd learned every shortcut, every alleyway that offered a quick escape. The city became my playground, and I was its reigning phantom.

One night, I had just finished a race-my bike screeching to a halt as I parked in an abandoned lot. I could hear the cheers from the crowd, the adrenaline still buzzing through my veins. As I removed my helmet and wiped sweat from my forehead, I could hear the whispers of awe and disbelief.

"Did you see that? Ghost was incredible tonight!" someone said, their voice filled with admiration.

"Yeah, she made that turn at insane speed. I thought for sure she was gonna crash!" another voice added.

The thrill of the race was more than just the speed; it was the thrill of the chase and the elusiveness of my new identity. I was a legend, and the stories of my daring moves spread faster than the rumors.

Meanwhile, the frustration in law enforcement was palpable.

Detective Ramirez was particularly frustrated. He had been assigned to crack the case of the elusive Ghost, but every attempt to catch her had ended in failure. His office was littered with reports, maps, and surveillance photos, all highlighting his ongoing battle with the anonymous rider.

"I swear, this Ghost is more slippery than a greased pig," Ramirez muttered to his partner, Officer Daniels, as he reviewed the latest footage from a security camera.

Daniels, leaning back in his chair, chuckled. "The whole city's buzzing about her. She's like some kind of urban legend. How the hell is she so good at evading us?"

Ramirez ran a hand through his hair, clearly exasperated. "She's got to have a pattern or something. We've got to figure out her next move. She's been pulling off these stunts for weeks, and every time we get close, she vanishes."

Their frustration was matched only by their fascination. The more they tried to catch her , the more they admired her skill. The chase had become a game, a puzzle that drove them both crazy.

In a dimly lit backroom of a local bar, a group of racing enthusiasts gathered, talking animatedly about Ghost.

"Man, have you seen her ride?" one of them said, his eyes wide with excitement. "She's like a machine, totally in control. It's insane."

"Yeah, and the cops can't touch her. It's like she's got some kind of sixth sense for avoiding them," another replied, shaking his head in disbelief.

Their conversations were filled with admiration and envy. I had become a symbol of freedom and defiance, someone who lived on the edge and defied the rules. To them, I was more than just a rider; I was a legend.

One night, as I prepared for another race, I felt a rush of exhilaration.

The thrill of being The Ghost was intoxicating, and the thrill of the chase was becoming my new normal. The city was mine to conquer, and every successful escape from the cops only added to it

As I revved the engine and prepared to launch into the night, I felt a sense of purpose that I hadn't felt since Jake's death. The darkness that had consumed me now fueled my every move, and the anonymity was a cloak I wore proudly. I was no longer just Emily; I was The Ghost, and the city was my playground.

The local news even picked up on Ghost.

"Who is this mysterious rider who's been evading the police for weeks?" the news anchor asked, her voice filled with intrigue. "Known only as 'Ghost,' this anonymous biker has taken the underground racing scene by storm. Law enforcement is baffled, and the public is fascinated. Stay tuned for more updates as we continue to follow this elusive figure."

It was a strange mix of empowerment and isolation. The city knew my name-Ghost-but no one knew the person behind the mask. The more I raced, the more the legend grew, and the more I embraced the darkness that had become my new reality.

Chapter 10

Ryan's POV:

I'd just moved to this city a couple of weeks ago, fresh off the force from a smaller town. The transition from sleepy suburbs to this bustling, gritty metropolis was jarring, but I was ready for the challenge. Little did I know that my initiation into this new city would come in the form of a phantom on two wheels.

It started with the chatter. Everywhere I went-coffee shops, bars, even the donut shop where I grabbed my morning fix-people were buzzing about this mysterious rider they called " Ghost." I heard whispers of her daring escapades and the frustration she caused among my colleagues. Naturally, I was intrigued.

My first real encounter with The Ghost was a late-night call. I was patrolling one of the city's more notorious areas when I saw a blur of black leather and chrome flash past me. My heart raced as I snapped on the lights and gave chase. The rider weaved through traffic with an impossible agility, slipping into alleys and evading every attempt I made to corner her. I had never seen such skill and audacity on the road.

"What the hell?" I muttered under my breath, trying to keep up. I knew I was outmatched. Ghost was a force of nature-each turn and acceleration a testament to her expertise. She disappeared into the night, leaving me with nothing but the roar of her engine echoing in the distance.

The more I learned about The Ghost, the more fascinated I became. My colleagues spoke of her with a mix of frustration and awe. They had been chasing her for weeks, but she remained an enigma. The local press had picked up on the story too, fueling the legend of the rider who could outwit the entire police department.

I started diving into everything I could find about her. The records showed numerous complaints and reports of her high-speed escapades, but not much more. She was elusive, almost mythical. Each report was like a breadcrumb leading me deeper into the mystery.

One evening, as I reviewed footage from security cameras, I saw her again. The footage was grainy, but I could still make out the sleek, black silhouette of her bike. The way she moved confident, precise was almost poetic. I was captivated. There was something hypnotic about her disregard for the rules and her mastery of the road.

"This is insane," I said aloud, more to myself than to anyone else. "She slips through every trap we set."

My fascination was more than professional; it was personal. I was drawn to her audacity, her ability to defy convention and live on the edge. The Ghost represented something raw and untamed, a stark contrast to the structured world of law enforcement I was used to.

I began following her rumored races, trying to get a sense of her patterns. Each time I saw her in action, I felt a mix of frustration and admiration. She was fearless, and her every move seemed to taunt us, daring us to catch her while simultaneously slipping away.

"Who are you?" I wondered aloud as I watched another race from the sidelines, the crowd's cheers a backdrop to my thoughts. "What drives you?"

The more I saw, the more I wanted to understand her. It wasn't just about catching her; it was about unraveling the mystery behind the legend. I was determined to get to know this rider who had captivated the city and eluded my colleagues for so long.

Every shift, every encounter, every chase only deepened my curiosity. I was drawn to The Ghost in a way I hadn't anticipated. It was like she had become a puzzle I was desperate to solve, and every failed attempt to capture her only fueled my determination to find out who she really was.

In my heart, I knew that catching The Ghost wasn't just about enforcing the law. It was about understanding the person behind the legend, and perhaps-just perhaps-finding a way to connect with a spirit that had become so elusive and enthralling.

Chapter 11

Ryan's POV:

I thought chasing down Ghost would be straightforward: catch the elusive rider, close the case, and move on. But that was before I'd actually seen her in action. Now, every encounter left me more fascinated and conflicted than the last.

Last night, I was on patrol near the city's industrial district when I caught sight of her. The familiar blur of black leather and roaring engine shot past me, and I immediately switched on the sirens. The chase was exhilarating and maddening all at once. She darted through the streets with a reckless precision that defied all logic. I pushed the limits of my cruiser, but she was always just out of reach.

"You've got to be kidding me!" I shouted to no one in particular as she slipped into a narrow alleyway, leaving me to deal with the mess of congested traffic. I felt like I was in a high-stakes game of cat and mouse, and I wasn't exactly winning.

The frustration was real, but so was the admiration. There was something magnetic about her-something that made me admire her audacity even as I was trying to apprehend her. She was a wild force of nature, and despite my duty to catch her, I found myself unable to stop thinking about her. Her skill, her style, the sheer defiance she exuded-it was all a bit intoxicating.

During a coffee break, I found myself explaining my fascination to Officer Daniels. He looked at me with a mix of amusement and skepticism.

"So, you're telling me you're actually starting to like Ghost?" he asked, taking a sip of his coffee.

"It's not that I like her, it's-" I struggled to find the words. "It's that I can't stop thinking about her. The way she rides, how she manages to outmaneuver everyone-it's like watching a high-speed ballet. It's impressive."

Daniels raised an eyebrow. "Impressive, huh? Sounds like you're developing a soft spot for her."

I rolled my eyes. "No, it's not like that. I just-there's something about her skill and her audacity that I can't ignore. She's a puzzle, and I want to figure her out."

The more I observed her, the more I found myself conflicted. On one hand, she was a lawbreaker, and I had a job to do. On the other hand, the way she lived on the edge was undeniably compelling. It was like she was challenging not just the law but the very concept of order and safety.

One evening, as I reviewed footage from a race, I couldn't help but chuckle at how seriously I was taking it.

The footage showed her effortlessly gliding around corners, the crowd's cheers in the background. I found myself laughing at the absurdity of it all. Here I was, a cop obsessing over an anonymous rider, and yet every time I saw her, I felt a thrill that went beyond professional curiosity.

"Alright, Ryan, get it together," I muttered to myself. "She's a criminal, not a rock star. Focus."

But the more I focused, the more I became intrigued. I started noticing little things-how she'd always take the same route through the alleyways, how she seemed to revel in the freedom she had on the road. It was like she was living in a world of her own making, and I was just an outsider trying to understand it.

One night, after yet another frustrating chase where she'd slipped through my fingers, I found myself talking to myself in the cruiser.

"Seriously, what is it with this woman?" I asked aloud, slumping in my seat. "She's like a combination of a ghost and a daredevil. It's impossible not to be impressed."

I shook my head and started the cruiser, heading back to the station. It was a frustrating night, but I couldn't deny the fact that my pursuit of Ghost had become more than just a job,it had become a personal mission to unravel the mystery behind her.

The more I saw of her, the more I realized that catching Ghost was not just about enforcing the law; it was about understanding the allure of the rider who had captivated the city, and, unexpectedly, me. It was a strange mix of admiration, frustration, and curiosity that kept me on her trail, even as I tried to reconcile my professional duty with the growing fascination I had for this mysterious and exhilarating figure on the road.

Chapter 12

Emily's POV:

Riding without a license plate had become more than just a form of rebellion; it was an adrenaline-fueled escape from the suffocating grief that seemed to follow me everywhere. The more I embraced my reckless side, the more the thrill of defying both the law and the expectations of society consumed me.

One night, I found myself racing through the city's underground circuit with a fervor I hadn't felt in months. The streets were mine-twisting, turning, and stretching out like an endless, dark highway. I leaned into every corner, pushing the bike to its limits. Each race was a new adventure, each risk a way to feel something beyond the pain.

During one particularly intense race, I narrowly avoided a collision.

I was overtaking a competitor when a car suddenly cut across my path. My heart pounded as I swerved, the tires screeching against the pavement. I managed to regain control, my pulse racing with the thrill of the near-miss.

"That was insane!" a fellow racer shouted as we pulled up to the finish line. His eyes were wide with admiration.

"Yeah, you almost had a head-on with that car," another added, shaking his head. "You're a madwoman, Ghost."

I grinned beneath my helmet, the compliment filling me with a twisted sense of pride. "Guess that's what makes it exciting."

The more reckless I became, the more I bonded with the underground racing crowd.

They admired my audacity and the way I seemed to dance on the edge of danger. In their eyes, I wasn't just a rider-I was a legend in the making. Their respect felt like a small, fleeting consolation for the void Jake had left behind.

One evening, as I sat on my bike with a group of racers, the conversation turned to my latest escapades.

"You've got guts, Ghost," one of them said, raising his beer in a toast. "Most people wouldn't dare take those kinds of risks."

I shrugged, trying to appear nonchalant. "I guess that's what keeps it interesting."

"Interesting doesn't even begin to cover it," another racer chimed in. "You're out there making history, and we're all here for it."

Their admiration fueled my need for danger. The more they cheered me on, the more I pushed the limits, constantly chasing that high that made me feel alive-if only for a little while.

Ryan's POV:

Watching Ghost from the sidelines was both frustrating and fascinating. I had seen her in action countless times now, and each encounter left me more intrigued by her audacity. Her reckless behavior had escalated, and it was clear she was pushing the boundaries even further.

I was on patrol one night when I caught sight of her again. She was racing through the city streets, weaving in and out of traffic with a nerve-wracking precision. I followed at a safe distance, knowing that trying to catch her would be futile. Her reckless maneuvers were both exhilarating and maddening to watch.

"She's pushing it to the limit tonight," I muttered to myself as I observed her from a few blocks away. The way she maneuvered through the chaos of the streets was almost artistic, and I couldn't deny the skill behind her defiance.

I heard through the grapevine that Ghost was the talk of the underground racing community.

In the break room at the station, I overheard a couple of officers discussing her latest exploits.

"Have you seen what Ghost pulled off last night?" one officer asked, shaking his head in disbelief.

"Yeah, I saw the footage," another replied. "The way she narrowly avoided that crash was insane. She's got some serious skills, no doubt."

The more I listened, the more I realized how much she had become a symbol of daring and defiance in the racing world. Her name was on everyone's lips, and the respect she commanded from fellow racers was undeniable.

Ghost's growing legend was both a challenge and a fascination.

As I drove through the city, the thought of her lingered in my mind. The more I observed her, the more I admired her bravery and the way she embraced the chaos. It was a rebellious spirit that I couldn't help but be drawn to, even as it conflicted with my duties as a cop.

Ghost was becoming more than just a target; she was an icon of rebellion, and my pursuit of her was turning into a deeper quest to understand the person who lived so fearlessly on the edge.

Chapter 13

Ryan's POV:

Catching The Ghost had turned into something personal. It wasn't just about duty anymore. It was about proving that I could outsmart this rider who had outwitted every cop in the city, including me. And deep down, it was about understanding what drove her to ride like she had nothing to lose.

I spent every spare moment studying her patterns. I mapped out her favorite routes, the alleys she used, and the spots where she liked to race. I knew I couldn't catch her by just following her-she was too damn good for that. I needed to anticipate her next move, to think like her.

"Alright, Ghost, let's see how well I've learned your tricks," I muttered, studying the map spread across my desk at the station.

That night, I set my plan in motion.

I positioned myself at a crossroads near one of her usual haunts, a place where she'd been known to race in the past.

The streets were quiet, but the tension in the air was palpable. I knew she'd be out tonight-I could feel it.

I kept my engine off, waiting. The streetlights cast long shadows across the pavement, and the city's noise hummed in the background. I was ready to spring into action the moment I saw her.

And then, like clockwork, I heard the distant roar of a motorcycle engine. My heart quickened as I recognized the sound. It was her.

I watched as she sped past me, the black leather of her jacket glinting under the streetlights. She was fast-so damn fast-but I was ready this time. I flipped on the engine and peeled out onto the street, keeping a safe distance. I wasn't going to scare her off; I was going to follow her, stay on her tail, and wait for the perfect moment to close in.

But as I tailed her, something strange happened. The thrill of the chase became intertwined with something else-an excitement I couldn't quite explain. It wasn't just about catching her anymore; it was about the chase itself. The way she rode, the way she danced on the edge of danger-it was exhilarating.

"Let's see where this road takes us," I whispered, my grip tightening on the wheel as I prepared to make my move.

Emily's POV

The wind in my face, the roar of the engine beneath me, the city lights blurring into streaks of color-it was pure, reckless freedom. Tonight, I felt unstoppable, like I could outrun any-thing, even the ghosts of my past.

But something was different tonight. I felt it in the pit of my stomach, a twinge of unease that I couldn't shake. Glancing in my mirror, I saw him-a cop, tailing me at a distance. I knew it was him. It had to be.

"Persistent, aren't you?" I muttered under my breath, a smirk tugging at the corner of my mouth.

This wasn't the first time he'd tried to catch me, but tonight, there was something more intense about the way he was following me. He wasn't just chasing me; he was hunting me. A part of me should've been scared, but instead, I felt a rush of adrenaline, a twisted sort of excitement that made my heart race even faster.

I leaned into the throttle, feeling the bike surge forward. The streets became a blur as I sped through them, weaving in and out of traffic, cutting through narrow alleys, trying to shake him off my tail. But no matter how fast I went, he was right there, keeping pace like a shadow I couldn't escape.

"Alright, if it's a chase you want, it's a chase you'll get," I said, my voice full of defiance as I pushed the bike even harder.

The city was my playground, and I knew every twist and turn by heart.

I darted through the maze of streets, cutting corners, taking sharp turns, and accelerating into the night. But he was relentless, matching me move for move. The thrill of it all was intoxicating-a game of cat and mouse where I was determined not to be caught.

The streets flashed by in a whirlwind of lights and shadows, and I could feel the tension building. It was like the world had narrowed down to just the two of us-the cop and The Ghost-locked in a dance that neither of us wanted to end.

As I took a sharp corner, I glanced in the mirror again and saw his car gaining on me.

"Damn it," I hissed, the realization hitting me that he was getting closer than ever before. But instead of panicking, I felt a twisted sort of thrill. The stakes were higher, the chase more intense, and I was riding that fine line between exhilaration and disaster.

"Come on, come on," I urged myself, weaving through traffic and darting into an alleyway. My heart was pounding in my chest, my thoughts racing as fast as the bike beneath me. I knew I couldn't keep this up forever, but I wasn't going to let him win-not tonight.

Ryan's POV

She was good-really good. But tonight, I was better. I kept my focus, navigating the twists and turns with a precision that surprised even me. Every move she made, I countered, staying just close enough to keep her in my sights.

When she ducked into an alleyway, I knew this was it-my chance to corner her. I followed, cutting off her exit just as she reached the end of the narrow passage. The adrenaline was pumping through my veins as I slammed on the brakes, blocking her path.

But she wasn't done yet. With a daring maneuver, she swerved, narrowly missing my cruiser and shooting back out onto the main street. I cursed under my breath, slamming the wheel in frustration, but I couldn't help but admire her tenacity.

"Not bad, Ghost. Not bad at all," I muttered, revving the engine and giving chase once more.

Emily's POV

My heart was in my throat as I barely escaped the cop's trap. He was good-too good. This wasn't just some rookie trying to score a collar; this was a man on a mission, and I was his target.

But the close call only fueled my resolve. I wasn't going to be taken down, not by him or anyone else. With a fierce determination, I tore through the city, every twist and turn a test of my skill and nerve.

As the night wore on, the chase became something more than just a game. It was a battle of wills, a test of who could outlast the other. I could feel the tension in the air, thick and electric, as we raced through the streets, both of us pushing ourselves to the limit.

Finally, after what felt like hours, I spotted an opening-a chance to disappear into the shadows where he couldn't follow. With one last burst of speed, I took the turn and vanished into the night, leaving him behind in the dark.

As I sped away, the adrenaline slowly began to fade, replaced by a mix of relief and exhilaration. I had escaped, but just barely. And I knew that he wasn't going to give up. He was going to keep coming after me, keep trying to catch me.

But as I rode through the empty streets, the city quieting down around me, I couldn't help but feel a twisted sort of satisfaction. The chase was on, and for the first time in a long time, I felt alive.

Chapter 14

Ryan's POV:

Tonight was different. There was a charge in the air, a buzzing energy that told me something big was about to go down. The city's usual noise seemed muted as I cruised through the streets, my senses heightened. Every night, I'd gotten closer to catching her-The Ghost-but she always slipped away at the last second. Tonight, though, felt like it could be the night I finally ended this chase.

I was parked near one of her favorite racing spots, a stretch of road just outside the city limits where the underground crowd loved to gather. The asphalt shimmered under the streetlights, reflecting the tension I felt in my gut. I'd been studying her moves, learning her patterns, and I was ready for her. The thrill of the chase had turned into something more-a relentless drive to match her, beat her at her own game.

And then, there she was.

I heard her before I saw her-the roar of that unmistakable engine, slicing through the quiet night like a blade. My heart rate kicked up as I spotted her in the distance, a shadow streaking through the city, defying the rules as always. I gripped the wheel, muscles tensing with the anticipation of what was to come.

"Alright, Ghost," I muttered under my breath. "Let's see what you've got tonight."

I hit the gas, the cruiser surging forward as I joined the chase. She was fast, maybe faster than I'd ever seen her. Her bike cut through the night like a phantom, darting through traffic with impossible precision. But I was ready, pushing my car to its limits to keep up. The city blurred around us as we weaved through the streets, the tension crackling in the air between us.

As I closed the gap, I could see her more clearly. The way she moved on that bike was mesmerizing-every shift of her weight, every lean into a curve was like a dance. It wasn't just skill; it was pure instinct, the kind of riding that came from deep within. And it only made me more determined.

She took a sharp turn, and I followed, tires screeching against the pavement. I was right on her tail now, and I could see her glancing back, just for a second. Our eyes met, and in that split moment, I felt a connection. It was like she was daring me, challenging me to keep up with her.

"Not this time," I whispered, pushing the car harder.

But just as I thought I had her, she pulled a move I hadn't seen coming. She cut through an alleyway, the narrow passage barely wide enough for her bike. I slammed the brakes, my cruiser skidding to a halt just in time. She had me again-damn it!

I reversed and shot down the street, trying to predict where she'd come out. She always had a backup plan, always knew how to use the city's layout to her advantage. I'd have to be smarter, faster, more cunning. My frustration grew, but so did my fascination. How could someone live so freely, so recklessly? It was like she didn't care about anything except the ride.

Emily's POV:

I could feel him behind me-his presence like a shadow I couldn't shake. The cop was good, better than I'd given him credit for. He'd been hunting me for weeks, getting closer each time. But tonight, something felt different. He wasn't just chasing me; he was in sync with me, almost like he could read my mind.

The thought sent a shiver down my spine, but it also fueled me. If he wanted a chase, I'd give him one he wouldn't forget.

I tore through the streets, every twist and turn a challenge to his pursuit. The night air was cool against my skin, the city lights flashing by in a blur. The adrenaline was coursing through me, and for the first time in a long while, I felt alive. There was something about being chased, being hunted, that made my heart race with excitement.

"Come on, you can do better than that," I whispered to myself, pushing the bike harder.

I glanced back, just for a second, and saw him-right on my tail. His face was set in determination, eyes locked on me like a predator. But there was something else there too, something that made my pulse quicken. He wasn't just a cop doing his job; he was invested, intrigued by the chase just as much as I was.

But I wasn't about to let him catch me. Not tonight.

I cut through an alleyway, the narrow space barely allowing my bike to squeeze through. It was a risky move, but it worked-his cruiser couldn't follow. I heard him skid to a halt behind me, and a thrill shot through me. I had him, again.

But I knew it wouldn't be for long. He'd be back on my trail in seconds, and I needed to stay ahead. I darted out onto another street, blending into the traffic, using the city as my camouflage. My heart was pounding, not just from the chase but from the thrill of outsmarting him yet again.

But deep down, I knew this couldn't last forever. He was getting better, faster, more determined. And a part of me didn't want it to end. There was something about this dance we were doing that made me feel connected to him, even though we were on opposite sides of the law.

As I sped through the city, my thoughts were racing just as fast. Who was this guy, this cop who seemed so fascinated by me? What drove him to keep chasing me, night after night? And why did it feel like I was starting to enjoy the chase just as much as he was?

Ryan's POV:

I roared back onto the main street, searching for any sign of her. She was a ghost in every sense of the word-here one second, gone the next. But I wasn't about to give up. I circled the area, scanning every alleyway, every intersection, looking for that one glimpse of her that would put me back in the game.

Finally, I saw her, a flash of black and chrome weaving through the traffic ahead. She hadn't shaken me after all. I hit the gas, adrenaline pumping as I closed the distance. She was good, but I was getting better.

The chase was on again, and this time, I was determined to end it. I could see her trying to lose me, but I was right there, matching her move for move. She had to know by now that I wasn't going to let her get away-not tonight.

As we raced through the city, the tension between us was electric. It was more than just a cop chasing a criminal; it was a clash of wills, of two people driven by something deeper than just the thrill of the ride. I could feel her spirit, her defiance, and it only made me want to catch her more.

"Not this time, Ghost," I whispered, my grip tightening on the wheel as I prepared to make my final move.

But as the night stretched on, I couldn't shake the feeling that this chase was more than just a pursuit of justice. It was something personal, something that made me question why I was so determined to catch her. Was it just about the thrill?

Or was it about understanding the woman behind the helmet, the one who lived so fearlessly on the edge?

Emily's POV:

He was closing in on me again, and I could feel the pressure mounting. My heart was pounding in my chest, but it wasn't just from the fear of being caught. There was something about this chase, about the way he was matching my every move, that sent a thrill through me.

I darted through another alley, the narrow walls closing in as I sped through. I knew he couldn't follow, but I also knew he'd be waiting for me when I emerged on the other side. He was smart, this cop-smarter than I'd given him credit for.

As I burst out onto the street again, I saw him, waiting for me, just as I'd predicted. But instead of panicking, I felt a rush of excitement. This wasn't just a chase anymore; it was a game, and I was determined to win.

"Let's see what you've got, officer," I whispered, leaning into the throttle and tearing down the street.

The city blurred around me as I pushed the bike to its limits, every sense heightened, every nerve on edge. The thrill of the chase was intoxicating, and for the first time, I realized that maybe, just maybe, I didn't want it to end.

As we raced through the city, the night stretching out before us, I felt a strange connection to the man chasing me. He wasn't just a cop; he was someone who understood the thrill of the ride, the danger, the freedom. And maybe that's

why I couldn't bring myself to hate him for trying to catch
me.

Because in the end, we were both chasing something.

Chapter 15

Emily's POV:

I walked into the small café on the corner of Maple and 5th, hoping to grab my usual cup of black coffee before the day really began. The bell above the door chimed as I entered, the familiar sound that always seemed to ease my nerves, even if just a little. The café was quiet, the early morning crowd thinning out, leaving only a few scattered patrons lost in their thoughts or their laptops.

I liked this time of day-the world was still waking up, and for a moment, everything felt almost normal. Almost. I shoved my hands into my jacket pockets, feeling the cool metal of my bike keys against my fingers. My mind kept drifting back to last night's chase, and the way that cop had nearly caught me. I could still feel the adrenaline, the thrill of it all. But there was something else too-a weird, unshakable feeling I couldn't quite pin down.

"Morning, Emily," the barista called, breaking me out of my thoughts. She was already reaching for the cup she knew I'd be asking for.

"Morning, Jess," I replied, forcing a smile. "The usual, please."

As Jess started making my coffee, I glanced around the room, taking in the quiet hum of the place. And then I saw him.

He was sitting at a table by the window, a cup of coffee in front of him, flipping through a newspaper. There was something familiar about the way he held himself, the way he was so focused on the page in front of him. It took me a second to recognize him, but when I did, my heart skipped a beat. It was him-the cop from last night. The one who'd almost caught me.

What the hell was he doing here?

I froze, my mind racing. Did he know who I was? Was he here because of me? But as I studied him, I realized he wasn't looking at me. He seemed completely engrossed in whatever he was reading, oblivious to my presence. Still, the sight of him sent a jolt through me, a weird mix of fear and curiosity.

I couldn't stay here. Not with him sitting so close. My mind was already working on a quick exit strategy when Jess called out, "Emily, your coffee's ready!"

I winced, knowing it was too late to make a quiet escape. The cop looked up at the sound of my name, his eyes scanning the room before landing on me. For a second, we just stared at each other, and I felt that same strange connection I'd felt during the chase. It was like he could see through me, see the secrets I was hiding. But then he smiled-a casual, friendly smile-and I felt the tension in my shoulders ease just a little.

"Thanks, Jess," I said, grabbing my coffee and heading for the door. But as I passed his table, I caught his eye again. There was something in his gaze that made me hesitate, made me feel like he was trying to figure something out.

"Morning," he said, his voice casual, but there was a hint of something else there too-like he was sizing me up.

"Morning," I replied, keeping my tone as neutral as possible. I was already halfway out the door when I heard him call after me.

"Hey, do you come here often?"

I paused, debating whether to answer or just keep walking. But something made me turn back, just for a second. "Sometimes," I said, trying to sound as uninterested as possible.

"Maybe I'll see you around, then," he said, that same smile still on his face.

I nodded, not trusting myself to say anything more, and quickly left the café. The cool morning air hit me as I stepped outside, and I took a deep breath, trying to calm the racing of my heart. What the hell was that? I couldn't believe I'd just had a conversation-no matter how brief-with the guy who'd been chasing me for weeks.

But as I walked down the street, coffee in hand, I couldn't shake the feeling that this wasn't over. Not by a long shot.

Ryan's POV:

I watched her as she left the café, a strange feeling settling in my chest. There was something about her that I couldn't quite place-something familiar. I couldn't stop thinking about the way her eyes had widened slightly when she first saw me, like she recognized me too. But from where?

As I took another sip of my coffee, I replayed our brief encounter in my mind. She'd been guarded, almost like she was trying to get away from me. But why? I couldn't shake the feeling that there was more to her than met the eye.

"Maybe I'll see you around," I'd said, but in my head, I was already planning how I could make sure of it. There was something about her that intrigued me, something that made me want to dig deeper.

And then it hit me-her name. Emily. I'd heard that name before, but where? I tried to remember if I'd come across it in any of the reports or files I'd been going through, but nothing came to mind. Still, I couldn't shake the feeling that I knew her from somewhere.

As I sat there, watching the spot where she'd just been, I couldn't help but think about Ghost. The thrill of the chase, the way she moved, the defiance in every turn she made. There was something about Emily that reminded me of her-of that same wild, untamed spirit that had drawn me to Ghost in the first place.

But that was ridiculous, right? Emily was just a woman grabbing her morning coffee. She couldn't possibly be the same person I'd been chasing through the city streets. And yet...

I shook my head, trying to clear the thought. It was too early to start jumping to conclusions. But as I finished my coffee and headed out, I couldn't help but keep an eye out for her. There was something about Emily that had grabbed my attention, and I wasn't about to let it go.

Maybe I would see her again. And maybe, just maybe, I'd figure out why I couldn't stop thinking about her.

Chapter 16

Emily's POV:

The night air was cool against my face, the wind whipping through my hair as I tore down the empty stretch of road. My bike roared beneath me, the engine's growl matching the chaos inside my head. The city lights blurred around me, transforming into streaks of color, but all I could focus on was the road ahead-always the road ahead.

I leaned into a turn, feeling the tires grip the asphalt, the familiar thrill shooting through me. But tonight, that thrill felt hollow. The usual rush that came with riding, with the freedom of it all, was tainted by something darker-something I couldn't shake, no matter how fast I went or how hard I pushed.

The memories hit me when I least expected them. Jake's laugh, that carefree grin he'd flash whenever he caught me staring at him. The way he used to call me "his girl" like it was the most natural thing in the world. I could hear his voice in my head, guiding me through that first ride, teasing me when I was too scared to take the turns at speed.

"Come on, Emily," he'd say with that lopsided smile. "You've got this. I'm right here."

But he wasn't here anymore. And that was the problem, wasn't it? I'd lost him. And with him, I'd lost a part of myself I didn't know how to get back.

I slowed down as I approached the edge of the city, the roar of the bike giving way to the silence of the night. There was a spot here-a quiet overlook where we used to come together. Jake loved it, the way the city lights stretched out below, the world seeming small and distant. It was our spot, our escape from everything.

I parked the bike and killed the engine, the sudden stillness almost deafening after the rush of the ride. I pulled off my helmet, letting the cool air hit my face as I stared out at the city. It was the same view, the same place, but everything felt different now.

I sank down onto the grass, my legs suddenly too heavy to hold me up. I could feel the tears threatening, the lump in my throat that I'd been trying to ignore for weeks. But out here, alone, I didn't have to hold it together. There was no one to see me fall apart.

The tears came slowly at first, hot and angry, as if they'd been waiting for this moment. And then all at once, they were pouring down my face, choking sobs that I couldn't stop. I buried my face in my hands, trying to muffle the sound, but it was no use. The grief was too much, too big to keep inside anymore.

"Jake," I whispered, the name slipping out like a prayer. "Why did you leave me?"

The silence that followed was unbearable. I waited for something-anything. A sign, a feeling, some sort of connection to him. But there was nothing. Just the cold night and the distant hum of the city below.

It wasn't supposed to be like this. We were supposed to have more time, more rides, more everything. I'd given up riding safely because what was the point? The only person who ever made me want to be careful, who made me believe there was something worth living for, was gone. And the person who took him from me? He was rotting in a cell, while I was out here, barely holding on.

I thought about the person I'd become-the Ghost. The reckless, fearless rider who tore through the streets with no regard for the rules. The girl who raced without a care, who didn't stop for anything or anyone. But was that really who I was? Or was it just the mask I wore to cover up the pain? The truth was, I didn't even know anymore.

I wanted to believe that this life, this wild, untamed freedom, was enough. But standing here, in the place that held so many memories of him, I couldn't lie to myself. It wasn't enough. And it would never be enough.

I thought about the racers who admired me, who saw me as this fearless leader, someone to look up to. They didn't know the truth-that every time I took off my helmet, I was just a scared girl running from a pain that wouldn't let go. They didn't know how many nights I'd spent here, in this spot, hoping that somehow, Jake would come back to me. They didn't know that every race, every reckless stunt, was my way of trying to feel something-anything-that wasn't this crushing grief.

But Jake wasn't coming back. And I was still here, trying to figure out what the hell I was supposed to do without him. The truth was, I didn't have a plan. I didn't have a reason. All I had was the bike and the road, and the desperate need to keep moving, because stopping hurt too damn much.

The thought of giving it all up crossed my mind-of walking away from the Ghost, from the races, from this life I'd built on the edge of destruction. But what else was there for me? My parents had abandoned me before I even had a chance to know them. I didn't have siblings, no one to ground me, no one to pull me back from the edge. And the one person who made me feel like I belonged somewhere was gone.

I squeezed my eyes shut, trying to push the memories away, but they kept coming, flooding my mind. The way Jake used to hold me, the way he'd look at me like I was the only person in the world that mattered. I'd never had that before him, and I knew I'd never have it again.

Maybe that was why I kept riding. Because as long as I was out there, as long as I was pushing the limits, I didn't have to think about what I'd lost. I didn't have to feel the emptiness that was swallowing me whole.

But now, sitting here, I realized something that scared me more than anything: I was losing myself too. I was becoming someone I didn't recognize, someone Jake wouldn't recognize. And I didn't know how to stop it.

I sat there for a long time, letting the tears come and go, letting the grief wash over me. The city lights flickered below, and the night wore on, but I couldn't bring myself to leave. Not yet.

When I finally stood up, the weight of my grief still clung to me, but there was something else there too-a small, fragile hope. Maybe I wasn't ready to give up the Ghost just yet. But I wasn't ready to let go of Jake either. I didn't know what that meant or what I was supposed to do next. But for the first time in a long time, I let myself hope that maybe, just maybe, there was a way to find myself again. Even if it meant facing the darkness head-on.

And with that, I turned back to my bike, the familiar weight of my helmet in my hands. I had no idea where the road would take me next, but I knew one thing for sure: I wasn't done fighting. Not yet.

Chapter 17

Ryan's POV:

I could feel it in my bones: today was going to be the day. I don't know why, but something about the way the morning sun was just starting to creep over the city, casting a golden hue over everything, made me believe that I was finally going to catch The Ghost. I was going to see who she really was beneath that helmet, the mysterious rider who had eluded me for so long.

I was getting too invested in this, I knew that. But it wasn't just about the job anymore. There was something about her-something wild and untamed-that I couldn't let go of. Maybe it was the way she rode, so fearless and free, like she had nothing left to lose. Or maybe it was the way she'd somehow managed to get under my skin without ever saying a single word to me.

As I walked into the station, I was greeted by the usual morning chaos-cops shuffling paperwork, the buzz of phones ringing, the low murmur of conversation. I nodded to a few of the guys as I headed for my desk, the stack of files waiting for me a grim reminder of just how much work there was to be done.

But even with all that, my mind was already on her-The Ghost. I couldn't stop thinking about her. Every time I closed my eyes, I saw her there, weaving through traffic, defying every law of physics with a grace that was almost impossible. And every time, I wondered what it would be like to finally see her face, to finally understand what drove her to ride the way she did.

I dropped into my chair and pulled up the latest report on my computer, the screen flickering to life with a map of the city. Red dots marked the places where The Ghost had been sighted in the past week-always moving, always just out of reach. It was like trying to catch smoke with my bare hands.

"She's like a damn ghost," I muttered to myself, shaking my head in frustration.

"Talking to yourself again, Ryan?" came a voice from behind me. I turned to see Officer Davis leaning against the door-frame, a cup of coffee in his hand and a smirk on his face.

"Maybe," I replied, not in the mood for his teasing this morning. "Just trying to figure out where she's gonna hit next."

Davis chuckled and shook his head. "Man, you've got it bad. I've never seen you this obsessed with a perp before. You sure it's just the thrill of the chase?"

I shot him a look, but he wasn't entirely wrong. I was obsessed, and not just because I wanted to catch her. There was something about The Ghost that was different from every other case I'd worked on. Something personal.

"It's just the job, Davis," I said, turning back to my screen. "And besides, no one else seems to be able to get close to her."

"Yeah, well, maybe that's because she's got you wrapped around her little finger," Davis said with a laugh. "Just be careful, man. Don't let this one get the best of you."

I waved him off, but his words stuck with me. Was I too close? Was I letting my fascination with The Ghost cloud my judgment? Maybe. But I couldn't help it. Every time she slipped through my fingers, I felt that much more determined to catch her. It wasn't just about winning-it was about understanding her, figuring out why she did what she did.

As the day wore on, I found myself growing more and more restless. I tried to focus on the paperwork in front of me, the endless stream of reports and statements, but my mind kept drifting back to The Ghost. Where was she now? What was she planning next? I couldn't stand the idea of just sitting here, waiting for her to make the next move.

So, I decided to change things up. Maybe I'd been going about this all wrong. I needed to start thinking like her, getting inside her head. If I could figure out what made her tick, maybe I'd have a better chance of predicting her next move.

I pulled out a map of the city, spreading it out across my desk, and started marking the locations of her last few sightings. There had to be a pattern here, something I was missing. I spent the next hour poring over the map, tracing routes, cross-referencing traffic cams, trying to piece together the puzzle.

But no matter how many times I went over it, the pattern eluded me. It was like she was deliberately unpredictable, hitting different parts of the city at random. It was frustrating as hell, but also... kind of genius.

I leaned back in my chair, rubbing a hand over my face. Maybe Davis was right. Maybe I was getting too close to this. But I couldn't back down now, not when I was so close. I had to find her, had to understand her. And maybe, just maybe, I had to see if there was something more to this than just the chase.

As I sat there, lost in thought, a sudden idea hit me. What if I changed my approach? I'd been trying to catch her by outsmarting her, but maybe that was the wrong way to go about it. Maybe I needed to do the opposite-make myself a target, draw her out. If I could get her to come to me, maybe I'd finally get the upper hand.

The more I thought about it, the more I liked the idea. It was risky, sure, but it might be my best shot. I started planning, going over the details in my head. I'd need to make sure everything was perfect-set up the right bait, create the right situation. And then, all I had to do was wait for her to take the bait.

It was a crazy plan, but then again, so was she. And maybe that was what made this whole thing so damn interesting.

By the time I left the station that evening, I had a plan in place. All I needed now was for her to show up. And something told me that she would.

As I drove home, my mind kept drifting back to her-the way she rode, the way she moved. There was something so captivating about it, something I couldn't put into words. I didn't know who she was or why she rode the way she did, but I knew one thing for sure: I had to find out.

And when I did, I wasn't sure if I wanted to arrest her... or something else entirely.

This chase was far from over. In fact, I had a feeling it was only just beginning.

Chapter 18

Ryan's POV:

It hit me like a ton of bricks, the realization that I was falling for her. Not just fascinated by her, not just obsessed with catching her, but actually falling for her. And the worst part? I didn't even know her real name.

I leaned against the hood of my patrol car, staring out at the city as the sun dipped below the horizon. The skyline was a wash of oranges and pinks, and usually, I'd find some peace in the view, but tonight, all I felt was conflicted. The city that stretched before me was hers as much as it was mine, maybe even more so. She owned these streets in a way that no one else did, and I couldn't help but be drawn to that-drawn to her.

But I was a cop, and she was the Ghost. The woman who defied every law, every rule, who made a mockery of everything I stood for. How the hell had I let it get to this point?

I closed my eyes, letting the cool evening air wash over me, trying to clear my head. But it was no use. She was always there, in the back of my mind. I could see her so clearly, the way she moved, the way she owned the road. There was something about her that got under my skin, something wild and untamed that called out to me. It wasn't just about the chase anymore. It was about her. And I hated myself for it.

"Damn it, Ryan," I muttered, running a hand through my hair in frustration. "What the hell are you doing?"

There was no answer, of course. Just the sound of the city waking up for the night, the distant hum of traffic, the occasional honk of a car horn. I should've been focusing on the case, on catching her, on doing my job. But all I could think about was how I felt when I saw her ride, how my heart raced every time she appeared in my sights.

I'd tried to push it down, to convince myself that it was just the thrill of the chase, that I was just a cop doing his job. But deep down, I knew it was more than that. The truth was, I was drawn to her in a way that terrified me. She was everything I wasn't-wild, reckless, free. And that scared the hell out of me.

I thought about the other night, the high-stakes chase that had ended with her slipping through my fingers once again. I'd been so close, so damn close, but she'd outmaneuvered me at the last second. And instead of feeling frustrated, all I could think about was how incredible she was, how much I wanted to know who she really was beneath that helmet.

I'd been lying to myself, pretending that this was all about the job. But I couldn't lie anymore. The truth was, I didn't just want to catch her. I wanted to know her. I wanted to understand what drove her, what made her tick. I wanted to see her face, hear her voice, feel that connection I knew was there, even if I couldn't explain it.

But that wasn't possible, was it? Because as much as I was falling for her, I was still a cop. And she was still a criminal. There was no future in that, no way to reconcile the two sides of my life. I couldn't be the man who loved her and the man who brought her in. One of those roles had to win out, and I wasn't sure which one it was going to be.

I pushed off the hood of the car, needing to move, to do something. Sitting still wasn't helping. I started pacing, my mind racing as I tried to figure out what the hell I was supposed to do. I couldn't keep going like this, couldn't keep letting her get to me. But I also couldn't walk away. I was too far gone for that.

I had to make a choice. And the more I thought about it, the more impossible it seemed. How could I choose between my duty and my heart? How could I give up one without losing a piece of myself?

I stopped pacing, my breath coming in short, sharp bursts. This wasn't just about catching the Ghost anymore. It was about finding out who I was-what kind of man I wanted to be. And that scared me more than anything.

I knew I was playing with fire. Falling for her was dangerous, reckless even. But I couldn't help it. I couldn't stop thinking about the way she made me feel, the way she made me question everything I thought I knew.

As the last light of the sun disappeared, leaving the city bathed in darkness, I made a silent vow to myself. I was going to find her. I was going to catch her. But when I did, it wasn't going to be just as a cop bringing in a criminal. It was going to be as a man who needed answers, who needed to know if there was something real between us.

Because as much as I tried to deny it, I knew the truth. I was falling for her-falling hard. And there was no turning back now.

Chapter 19

Emily's POV:

The engine roared beneath me, the vibration of the bike coursing through my body as I tore down the highway. The night air was cool against my skin, but it did nothing to calm the storm raging inside me. I was The Ghost, the one who defied the rules, who lived on the edge, who made the streets my playground. But as the city blurred past me, the familiar rush of adrenaline felt hollow, like an echo of something that used to mean so much more.

I used to ride for Jake. I used to ride because it made me feel alive, because it was something we shared. But now? Now I wasn't sure why I was still doing it. The thought crept in like an unwanted guest, and no matter how fast I went, I couldn't outrun it.

What the hell was I doing?

I slowed the bike to a crawl, pulling off to the side of the road. The city lights twinkled in the distance, a beautiful, chaotic mess that felt worlds away. I killed the engine and sat there in the silence, the only sound the soft ticking of the cooling metal and my own uneven breathing. The helmet felt suffocating, a barrier between me and the rest of the world. I yanked it off, letting it drop to the ground beside me.

I stared out at the skyline, the familiar ache in my chest growing stronger by the second. This was supposed to make me feel better, supposed to make me forget. But all it did was remind me of how lost I really was.

Jake would hate this. He'd hate what I'd become, what I was doing. And that thought hurt more than anything else. He was the reason I'd stayed safe, stayed sane. Without him, everything felt meaningless, like I was just going through the motions, trying to fill a void that could never be filled.

I closed my eyes, leaning forward until my forehead rested against the handlebars. Memories of Jake flooded my mind-his smile, the way he used to look at me, like I was the only person in the world who mattered. The way he used to hold me after a long ride, his arms warm and safe, a reminder that I wasn't alone.

But I was alone now. So alone. And the one thing that had always brought me comfort, that had made me feel close to him, was starting to feel like a lie.

Tears welled up in my eyes, and I didn't bother to wipe them away. What was the point? No one was here to see me fall apart. No one cared. No family, no one. Except Jake. And he was gone.

I'd been running for so long, trying to escape the pain, trying to pretend that I was still in control, that I was still the same person I was before. But I wasn't. I hadn't been for a long time. And the more I rode, the more I realized that this wasn't filling the void. It was only making it bigger.

"What am I doing, Jake?" I whispered into the night, my voice barely audible. "Why am I still doing this?"

But there was no answer. There never was. Just the empty silence and the weight of my own grief pressing down on me, suffocating me.

I thought about the races, the illegal runs that had become my life, my identity. The thrill of being The Ghost, of being untouchable, anonymous. It had felt good at first, like I was invincible. But now, it felt like a mask I couldn't take off, a role I was trapped in. I didn't even know who I was anymore, without the bike, without the helmet. Was there anything left of Emily? Or was she just a ghost too?

The wind picked up, rustling the leaves in the trees, carrying with it the distant sounds of the city. I wondered if anyone else out there felt like this-so lost, so broken. It was hard to imagine that they did. Everyone else seemed to have it together, seemed to know who they were, what they wanted. But me? I didn't even know what I was running from anymore. Or what I was running towards.

I looked down at the bike, the sleek machine that had become an extension of myself. It had been my escape, my salvation. But now, it just felt like a reminder of everything I'd lost, everything I couldn't get back. Jake, my future, my sense of purpose. It was all gone, and I was just going through the motions, pretending that this was enough.

But it wasn't. It never would be.

I couldn't keep living like this, couldn't keep pretending that I was okay. I wasn't okay. I was falling apart, and there was no one left to catch me.

"What do I do now, Jake?" I asked, my voice breaking. "Where do I go from here?"

But the night gave no answers, just the empty echoes of my own voice. I was on my own, and the path ahead was as dark and uncertain as the road stretching out before me.

I took a deep breath, trying to steady myself, trying to find some kind of clarity. But all I felt was the crushing weight of my own grief, the overwhelming sense that I had nothing left to lose.

And maybe that was the scariest part. Because when you have nothing left to lose, you stop caring. You stop trying. And that's when you really become lost.

I stood up, leaving the helmet on the ground, and climbed back onto the bike. The engine roared to life beneath me, but it didn't feel the same. It didn't feel like freedom. It felt like chains, like a burden I couldn't shake.

I revved the engine and took off down the road, the city lights blurring around me. But no matter how fast I went, no matter how far I rode, I couldn't escape the truth.

I was lost. And I didn't know if I'd ever find my way back.

Chapter 20

R yan's POV:

The streets were quiet tonight, quieter than usual. The kind of quiet that makes you uneasy, like the city itself is holding its breath, waiting for something to happen. And maybe it was. Maybe it was waiting for me to finally make up my damn mind about what I was going to do.

I'd been chasing The Ghost for months, but it wasn't just about the thrill of the pursuit anymore. Somewhere along the line, this chase had become something else-something personal. She wasn't just a faceless rider anymore. She was someone I needed to understand, someone who had gotten under my skin in a way I couldn't shake.

I leaned back in my chair at the station, staring at the map of the city plastered on the wall in front of me. Red pins marked the spots where she'd been sighted, like a trail of breadcrumbs scattered across the urban landscape. But there was no pattern, no logic to her movements. She rode where she wanted, when she wanted, and no one had been able to predict her next move.

Including me.

I sighed, running a hand through my hair. It was getting late, and the station was almost empty, the fluorescent lights casting a harsh glow over the empty desks and stacks of paperwork. I should have gone home hours ago, but how could I? The Ghost was out there somewhere, riding through the night, and I was no closer to catching her than I'd been on day one.

But maybe that was the problem. I'd been so focused on catching her, on outsmarting her, that I hadn't stopped to ask myself the most important question: why? Why was she doing this? What was driving her to take these insane risks, to live on the edge like this?

I needed to know. Not as a cop, but as a man who couldn't stop thinking about her, couldn't stop wondering what kind of person she really was underneath that helmet.

I grabbed my jacket off the back of the chair and headed for the door, my footsteps echoing in the empty hallway. I had no plan, no strategy. Just a gut feeling that I needed to confront her, to talk to her, to see if there was something more behind those wild eyes and reckless stunts.

As I stepped out into the cool night air, I felt a strange sense of calm settle over me. I wasn't going out there as Officer Ryan King tonight. I was just Ryan, a guy who needed answers, who needed to understand this woman who had turned his life upside down.

I climbed into my car and started the engine, the familiar rumble grounding me as I pulled out of the parking lot. I had a pretty good idea of where she might be tonight. The Ghost had her favorite spots, places where she could push the limits without too much interference.

It didn't take long to find her. I spotted her before she saw me, her bike idling at the edge of a deserted overpass, the city lights stretching out like a glittering sea below. She was alone, her silhouette dark against the glow of the skyline, and for a moment, I hesitated.

But I couldn't turn back now. I needed to do this.

I parked a little ways off, making sure to approach on foot so I wouldn't spook her. As I got closer, I could see that she was just sitting there, staring out at the city, her helmet cradled in her hands. The sight struck me like a punch to the gut. She looked so small, so vulnerable, nothing like the fearless Ghost who had outmaneuvered me time and time again.

I took a deep breath and stepped forward, my voice low and steady. "I didn't come here to arrest you."

She didn't move, didn't even flinch. For a moment, I wondered if she'd even heard me. But then she spoke, her voice quiet, tinged with something I couldn't quite place.

"Then what do you want?"

I walked closer, stopping a few feet away from her. "I want to understand. I want to know why you're doing this."

She let out a bitter laugh, shaking her head. "You think you can understand me? Just like that?"

I shrugged, trying to keep my tone gentle. "Maybe. If you give me a chance."

She finally looked at me, her eyes locking onto mine, and the intensity in her gaze took my breath away. There was pain there, deep and raw, mixed with something that looked an awful lot like anger.

"You don't know anything about me," she said, her voice tight.

"No," I admitted. "I don't. But I want to. I want to know who you are when you're not wearing that helmet. I want to know what's driving you to take these risks, to live like every day is your last."

She stared at me for a long time, her expression unreadable. Then, slowly, she put the helmet back on and started the bike, the engine growling to life.

"You're too late," she said over the roar. "You're too late to save me."

With that, she tore off into the night, leaving me standing there, feeling more lost than ever. But as I watched her disappear into the darkness, I knew one thing for certain.

I wasn't going to give up. I was going to find her, talk to her, and try to understand what had turned her into Ghost. And maybe, just maybe, I could find a way to save her from whatever demons were chasing her.

Because no matter how much she pushed me away, no matter how many walls she put up, I couldn't stop myself from caring. And that was the most terrifying realization of all.

Chapter 21

Ryan's POV:

The night was thick with tension, the air heavy as I patrolled the city streets, my mind consumed by thoughts of her. The Ghost. Emily. The girl I couldn't stop thinking about. The one who had become more than just a target, more than just another reckless rider. She was a mystery, a puzzle I was desperate to solve.

And tonight, I was going to find her.

I had been following her trail for weeks, getting closer and closer, but always one step behind. But tonight, something felt different. Maybe it was the way the air hummed with electricity, or the fact that I had a gut feeling this was it. This was the night I would finally confront her.

I drove through the familiar streets, my eyes scanning every corner, every alleyway. The city was alive with its usual chaos—horns blaring, people shouting, lights flashing—but I tuned it all out, focused on the one thing that mattered.

Then I saw her.

She was riding fast, weaving through traffic with the kind of reckless abandon that both thrilled and terrified me. But this time, I was ready. I knew her moves, her patterns. I knew how she thought.

I hit the gas, the engine roaring as I sped after her. The chase was on, but this time I wasn't letting her slip away. Not again.

She glanced over her shoulder, spotting me, and I saw the moment she realized I was onto her. Her bike accelerated, and I matched her speed, weaving through the same tight gaps in traffic, my heart pounding with adrenaline.

We raced through the city, the streets a blur of lights and shadows. I could feel the tension in the air, a palpable thing between us as we pushed our bikes to the limit. But this wasn't just another chase. This was personal. I needed to catch her, to talk to her, to finally understand what had driven her to this.

We tore down a side street, the buildings closing in around us. I could see the desperation in her movements, the way she was trying to shake me off. But I wasn't backing down. Not tonight.

She swerved sharply, taking a sudden turn down a deserted alley. I followed, the narrow walls echoing with the roar of our engines. My breath was coming in short, sharp bursts, my entire body focused on the chase.

And then, just like that, it was over.

The alley dead-ended, and she skidded to a stop, her bike coming to a halt in a cloud of dust and gravel. I was right behind her, pulling up and killing the engine before she could make a move.

For a moment, we just sat there, the only sound the ticking of cooling engines and our heavy breathing. The tension was thick, almost suffocating, as we faced each other in the dim light of the alley.

Then she swung off her bike, ripping off her helmet and throwing it to the ground with a frustrated growl. Her hair tumbled out, wild and untamed, framing a face that was a mixture of anger, pain, and something else—something that hit me right in the gut.

I climbed off my bike and approached her slowly, my hands held out in a gesture of peace. "I'm not here to arrest you," I said, my voice calm but firm. "I just want to talk."

She glared at me, her chest heaving with emotion. "What do you want from me?" she demanded, her voice raw. "Why can't you just leave me alone?"

"Because I care," I shot back, more forcefully than I intended. "I've been chasing you for months, and it's not just because it's my job. It's because I need to understand why you're doing this. Why you're risking your life every night."

She looked away, her jaw clenched tight, as if she was trying to hold back the storm of emotions threatening to break free. "You wouldn't understand," she muttered.

"Then help me understand," I urged, taking a step closer. "Tell me what's going on, Emily. Tell me why you've turned into The Ghost."

At the mention of her name, she stiffened, her eyes flashing with a mix of surprise and pain. But she didn't deny it. Instead, she took a deep breath, and when she spoke again, her voice was softer, tinged with the weight of memories.

"You really want to know?" she asked, her tone almost a challenge.

I nodded, my heart pounding in my chest. "Yes."

She closed her eyes for a moment, as if gathering the strength to speak. When she opened them again, they were filled with a sadness that took my breath away.

"I wasn't always like this," she began, her voice quiet, almost distant. "I used to be... happy. Or at least, I thought I was. But everything changed when Jake died."

Her words hung in the air between us, heavy with the weight of loss. I didn't interrupt, sensing that this was something she needed to get out, something she hadn't shared with anyone in a long time.

"He was my everything," she continued, her voice trembling. "He taught me how to ride, how to love the freedom of the open road. We were supposed to have a future together. But then... he was taken from me."

I saw the tears welling up in her eyes, but she blinked them back, her expression hardening as she continued. "After he died, I didn't know how to cope. I couldn't face the world without him, so I started riding. Fast, reckless, like I didn't care if I lived or died. Because I didn't."

Her voice broke, and she looked away, struggling to keep her composure. I felt a deep ache in my chest as I watched her, understanding now the pain that had driven her to this point.

"Becoming The Ghost was my way of escaping," she said, her voice barely above a whisper. "I didn't want to be Emily anymore, because Emily was broken, shattered. But The Ghost? She was fearless. She didn't have to feel anything. She could just ride and forget."

For a moment, neither of us spoke, the silence filled with the echoes of her confession. I could see now why she had been running, why she had embraced this dangerous, reckless life. But I also saw the toll it had taken on her, the way it had consumed her, leaving her more lost and broken than ever.

"I'm sorry," I said softly, the words feeling inadequate, but it was all I could offer. "I'm so sorry for what you've been through."

She met my gaze, and for the first time, I saw a flicker of something other than pain in her eyes. Maybe it was relief, or maybe it was just exhaustion, but whatever it was, it made me want to reach out to her, to hold her and tell her that she wasn't alone anymore.

But I knew that wouldn't be enough. She needed more than just sympathy. She needed a way out, a way to heal, and I wasn't sure I could give that to her. But I wanted to try.

"What if you didn't have to be The Ghost anymore?" I asked gently. "What if you could find a way to be Emily again?"

She looked at me, a mix of fear and uncertainty on her face. "I don't know if I can," she admitted. "I don't even know who Emily is anymore."

I stepped closer, closing the distance between us. "Then let me help you find her," I said, my voice filled with a determination I hadn't felt in a long time. "You don't have to do this alone, Emily. You don't have to keep running."

She stared at me, and I could see the conflict in her eyes, the battle between the part of her that wanted to believe me and the part that was too scared to hope.

Finally, she nodded, a small, tentative movement, but it was enough.

"Okay," she whispered, her voice barely audible. "Okay."

And in that moment, I knew that this was the turning point. Not just for her, but for both of us. Because no matter what happened next, I wasn't going to let her face it alone.

Chapter 22

Emily's POV:

The night was heavy, the kind that pulls you down, forces you to confront the darkest parts of yourself. I could feel the weight of Ryan's eyes on me, waiting, urging me to open up. Part of me wanted to run, to throw on my helmet and ride away until the pain was nothing but a distant hum. But the other part, the part that had started to trust him, knew that running wasn't going to make it stop.

So I took a deep breath, bracing myself against the raw memories clawing at the edges of my mind.

"It was a year ago," I began, my voice trembling despite my efforts to stay composed. "Jake and I... we were everything to each other. He was the one who taught me how to ride, you know? He always said that life was meant to be lived at full speed, but only if you had someone to ride alongside you."

I paused, the memory of Jake's smile flashing in my mind. God, I missed that smile. The way it lit up his face, the way it made me feel like nothing could go wrong as long as we were together.

"He was careful, though," I continued, my throat tightening. "For all his talk of speed, Jake was the kind of guy who made sure his helmet was on just right, that his bike was in perfect condition. He never took unnecessary risks. We promised each other that we'd always ride safe... for each other's sake."

I could see the questions in Ryan's eyes, but he didn't interrupt. He just stood there, silently urging me to go on, his presence steady and unyielding, like a lifeline.

"Then one day, we were out on the road, just like any other day," I said, my voice cracking. "We were riding through the countryside, the wind in our faces, everything perfect. And then... it wasn't."

I bit down on my lip, the pain sharp enough to keep the tears at bay. "There was this truck," I forced out. "It came out of nowhere, speeding right at us. Jake tried to swerve, tried to avoid it, but..."

I broke off, the image of that day seared into my mind. The screech of tires, the crunch of metal, Jake's bike skidding out of control. The sickening thud as he hit the ground.

"The driver didn't even stop," I whispered, the anger burning through my grief. "He just kept going, like Jake's life didn't matter. Like we didn't matter."

I could feel the tears now, hot and angry, sliding down my cheeks. "I held him, Ryan. I held him as he took his last breath. And I couldn't do a damn thing to save him."

I looked up at Ryan then, half-expecting to see pity in his eyes. But all I saw was a deep, quiet empathy, a shared pain that made my heart ache even more.

"After that, I didn't know who I was without him," I admitted, my voice small. "I couldn't bear to ride the way we used to, so I became someone else. Someone who didn't care if she lived or died. I became The Ghost, because it was easier to disappear than to face the reality that Jake was gone."

Ryan stepped closer, his hand reaching out to gently touch my arm. "Emily, I'm so sorry," he said, his voice filled with a sincerity that made it hard to breathe. "I can't imagine what you went through, what you're still going through."

I looked away, the tears still falling despite my best efforts to stop them. "I didn't want to feel anything anymore," I said, my voice barely a whisper. "So I shut it all out, pushed everyone away. But then you... you wouldn't let me."

He moved even closer, his hand now resting on my shoulder, grounding me in a way I hadn't felt in a long time. "You don't have to be The Ghost anymore, Emily," he said softly. "You don't have to carry this alone. Let me help you. Let me be here for you."

I searched his eyes, looking for any sign of doubt, but all I saw was a quiet determination, a promise that he wasn't going to give up on me.

"But I'm a mess," I said, the words slipping out before I could stop them. "I'm broken, Ryan. I don't know how to be anything else."

He shook his head, his grip on my shoulder tightening. "You're not broken, Emily. You're hurt, you're grieving, but you're not broken. And you don't have to go through this alone. I'm here, and I'm not going anywhere."

His words, his presence, it was too much. The walls I had built up started to crumble, and for the first time since Jake died, I let myself feel the full weight of my grief. I collapsed against Ryan, the sobs wracking my body as I finally let it all out.

And he held me. He held me like I was something precious, something worth saving. And for the first time in a long time, I started to believe that maybe, just maybe, I was.

Ryan's POV

Holding Emily in my arms as she broke down, I felt a fierce protectiveness rise up in me, a need to be there for her, to help her carry this unbearable burden. I had been drawn to her from the moment I saw her on that bike, the way she defied the world with every reckless turn. But now, knowing what drove her, knowing the pain she carried, my feelings had deepened into something more. Something I wasn't ready to name, but something that was undeniably there.

I could feel her shaking against me, her sobs slowly subsiding as the storm of emotions began to pass. But I didn't let go. I wasn't going to let go until she knew, without a doubt, that she wasn't alone.

"Emily," I whispered, my voice hoarse from the intensity of the moment. "I'm here. I've got you."

She pulled back slightly, just enough to look up at me, her eyes red and swollen but filled with a kind of fragile hope. "Why?" she asked, her voice trembling. "Why do you care so much?"

I didn't have a simple answer for that. I didn't even fully understand it myself. All I knew was that from the moment I laid eyes on her, from the moment I saw that first flicker of pain in her eyes, something inside me had shifted. I wasn't just a cop trying to catch a reckless rider anymore. I was a man who had found something worth fighting for, worth protecting.

"Because I see you," I said finally, the words coming out more honest than I expected. "Not just The Ghost, not just the girl who rides like she's got nothing to lose. I see *you*, Emily. And I care because I know what it's like to lose something, to feel like there's nothing left. But you do have something left. You have a future, and I want to help you find it."

Her eyes searched mine, as if trying to decide if she could trust me, if she could let me in. I held her gaze, willing her to see that I wasn't going anywhere, that I was in this for the long haul.

"I'm scared," she admitted, her voice small, vulnerable.

"I know," I said, my heart aching for her. "But you don't have to be scared alone. We can face this together."

For a moment, she just stared at me, and I could see the battle playing out behind her eyes-the fear, the doubt, but also the hope. And then, slowly, she nodded.

"Okay," she whispered, her voice barely audible. "Together."

And in that moment, I knew that this was just the beginning. The beginning of something real, something worth fighting for. And no matter what came next, I was ready. Because I had found something in Emily that I hadn't even known I was looking for. And I wasn't going to let it slip away.

Chapter 23

Emily's POV:

The days after our confrontation were a whirlwind of emotions, a strange mix of hope and trepidation. Ryan and I began to navigate the fragile territory between us, moving cautiously but with a shared determination to heal and find a semblance of normalcy.

Our meetings started out simple. Coffee at a local café, where we'd sit for hours, talking about anything and everything. It was during these moments that I felt a kind of peace I hadn't experienced in a long time. The ordinary, everyday conversations helped ground me, helped me remember that life could be mundane and beautiful all at once.

One afternoon, as we sat in our favorite booth at the café, I stirred my coffee absentmindedly, watching Ryan over the rim of my mug. He was talking animatedly about a case he'd been working on, his eyes bright and his gestures animated. I couldn't help but smile at his enthusiasm. It was a side of him I was getting to know, a side that was so different from the determined cop who had been chasing The Ghost.

"You know," he said, breaking my reverie, "I used to think that being a cop was all about catching the bad guys. But it's more than that. It's about understanding people, helping them in ways that go beyond just enforcing the law."

I nodded, taking in his words. "I've seen that in you," I admitted. "You're not just about catching The Ghost. You're about finding out who she is, why she's hurting. It's... different."

He looked at me, a small, genuine smile playing at his lips. "It's because of you," he said softly. "You've made me see things differently. I've learned that understanding someone's pain can be more important than anything else."

The sincerity in his voice touched me deeply. For the first time in a long time, I felt like I was being seen for who I truly was, not just the persona I had created as The Ghost. It was a revelation that made me want to open up even more, to let him in further.

We started taking long walks together, exploring new parts of the city that neither of us had seen before. The walks became our therapy, our way of processing everything we were going through. We talked about our pasts, our dreams for the future, and the things that scared us. It was during these walks that I felt a genuine connection forming, one that was rooted in mutual respect and understanding.

One evening, as the sun began to set and the city lights started to twinkle, we found ourselves on a quiet bridge overlooking the river. The view was breathtaking, the water shimmering under the fading light. We leaned against the railing, the cool breeze brushing against our faces.

"I used to come here with Jake," I said, my voice soft. "We'd sit here and talk about our plans, our dreams. It was one of our favorite spots."

Ryan turned to me, his expression a mix of curiosity and empathy. "What did you talk about?"

I hesitated for a moment, then began to share the memories that had been both painful and comforting. "We talked about everything," I said. "Our future, the kind of life we wanted to build together. We even joked about opening a little motor-cycle shop someday, you know? A place where people could come for repairs and advice. It was a silly dream, but it was ours."

Ryan listened intently, his gaze steady and reassuring. "That doesn't sound silly at all," he said. "It sounds like a beautiful dream. And maybe, even though Jake isn't here, you can still hold on to that dream. You don't have to let it go just because he's not here."

His words struck a chord deep within me. I had spent so long burying my dreams and memories with Jake, convinced that letting go was the only way to move forward. But maybe, just maybe, there was a way to honor those dreams while still finding a new path for myself.

"You really think so?" I asked, a hint of vulnerability in my voice.

"I do," Ryan said, his tone sincere. "I think Jake would want you to live your life fully, to pursue your dreams, even if they're different from what you once imagined. And I want to help you do that."

His support was like a beacon in the darkness, guiding me toward a future I had almost given up on. With Ryan by my side, I started to see a glimmer of hope in the distance, a possibility that life could be meaningful and fulfilling again.

We also spent time working together on projects that helped us process our grief and move forward. One weekend, we volunteered at a community center, helping with a charity event. It was a small gesture, but it felt significant. For me, it was a way to reconnect with a sense of purpose, to give back in a way that honored Jake's memory. For Ryan, it was a chance to be more than just a cop, to make a positive impact in a different way.

Ryan's POV

Watching Emily open up, seeing her begin to reclaim parts of herself that had been lost in the wake of Jake's death, was both inspiring and heartbreaking. Each step she took toward healing was a testament to her strength, and it made me want to be there for her in every way possible.

Our time together was filled with moments of laughter and reflection, but it was also marked by a deep, unspoken understanding. Emily was slowly letting go of The Ghost, letting go of the need to hide behind that mask of indifference. And I was here to support her, to stand by her as she rediscovered who she was without Jake.

One night, as we sat together on the bridge overlooking the river, I couldn't help but feel a sense of gratitude for the chance to be part of her journey. We were no longer just two people caught in a chase. We were two people healing, learning to navigate the complexities of our emotions and our pasts.

"I know this is a lot to ask," I said quietly, breaking the silence. "But I want to be here for you, not just as a cop, but as a friend. And maybe more than that. I don't know what the future holds, but I do know that I want to be part of it."

Emily looked at me, her eyes reflecting the colors of the sunset. There was a softness in her gaze that I hadn't seen before, a hint of the vulnerability she had been carrying for so long.

"I appreciate that," she said, her voice steady but filled with emotion. "And I want you to know that I'm trying. I'm trying to find myself again, to make peace with the past and look forward to the future. Having you here, it means more to me than you know."

Her words touched me deeply, and I felt a surge of affection for her that went beyond the physical attraction I had initially felt. It was a profound connection, one that was built on shared pain and mutual support.

"I'm glad to hear that," I said, reaching out to gently touch her hand. "Because I'm here for the long haul. Whatever you need, whatever you want, I'll be by your side."

As we sat together, watching the sunset paint the sky in shades of orange and pink, I felt a sense of peace that I hadn't felt in a long time. The road ahead was still uncertain, but with Emily by my side, I knew that we could face it together.

In helping her find her way, I was also finding my own. And maybe, just maybe, this was the beginning of something beautiful and transformative for both of us.

Chapter 24

Emily's POV

The sense of calm I'd been clinging to was soon shaken by the arrival of unexpected challenges. Just when I thought I was finding my footing, the remnants of my past began to resurface, threatening to unravel the fragile stability I had worked so hard to build.

It started with a knock on my door late one evening. I opened it to find a scruffy man in his early forties, his eyes shadowed by a battered cap. He introduced himself as one of Jake's old acquaintances, someone I barely remembered. But his presence was enough to send a shiver down my spine.

"I need to talk to you," he said, his tone serious. "It's about Jake. There are things you need to know."

I let him in, though I was wary. We sat in the dimly lit living room, the silence heavy with unspoken tension. He started to speak, revealing unsettling details about the circumstances surrounding Jake's death. Apparently, the truck driver wasn't just some random criminal; he had connections to a larger, more dangerous network. And now, with the case being reopened, there were whispers of revenge and unfinished business.

I felt like the ground was slipping from under me. All the progress I'd made in accepting Jake's death and moving forward was being overshadowed by a shadowy past that I couldn't escape. The memories of that fateful day came rushing back, along with a paralyzing fear that I might once again be caught in a web of violence and danger.

Ryan's POV

When Emily called me that night, her voice trembling, I knew something was wrong. I rushed over to her apartment, my heart pounding with concern. Seeing her there, looking lost and frightened, I felt a surge of protectiveness.

"Hey, what's going on?" I asked as I stepped inside. The atmosphere was tense, and I could sense the unease in the room.

Emily glanced at me, her eyes filled with worry. "I just had someone from Jake's past show up. He's talking about some dangerous connections and... I don't know what to do."

I took a deep breath, trying to stay calm. "Alright, let's talk this through. I'm here for you, and we'll figure this out together."

Emily nodded, though her face was pale. She explained the situation, detailing the stranger's claims and the fear that had gripped her. I listened carefully, piecing together the puzzle of her past and the new threats that had emerged.

"You're not alone in this," I assured her. "I'll help you deal with whatever's coming. We'll take it step by step, and we'll make sure you're safe."

Emily's POV

The following days were a blur of anxiety and confusion. The man's warnings had set off a chain reaction, bringing unwanted attention to my life. I started noticing strange cars parked outside my apartment, people who seemed to be watching me from a distance. The paranoia was suffocating, and I found myself on edge, unable to relax.

Ryan was a constant presence during this time, his support unwavering. We spent hours researching and strategizing, trying to understand the scope of the danger and how to protect myself. He reached out to contacts in law enforcement to get a clearer picture of what we were dealing with.

One evening, as we sat at my kitchen table surrounded by stacks of notes and files, Ryan looked at me with a determined expression. "We'll get through this," he said, his voice steady. "I know it's scary right now, but we're not facing this alone. I've got your back, and we'll figure out how to handle whatever's coming."

I looked at him, grateful for his unwavering support. "I don't know what I'd do without you," I said, my voice breaking slightly. "You've been more than I ever expected, and I'm scared of what might happen."

He reached out and took my hand, his touch warm and reassuring. "You're stronger than you know, Emily. And together, we'll face whatever comes our way."

Ryan's POV

Watching Emily struggle with the resurgence of danger in her life was heart-wrenching. The resilience she had shown in her journey to heal was now being tested by external threats that seemed almost insurmountable. But if there was one thing I had learned from getting to know her, it was that she was tougher than she gave herself credit for.

We spent countless hours tracking down leads and working with the authorities to understand the network that had been involved in Jake's death. It was clear that this was no ordinary case; there were powerful forces at play, and Emily was at the center of it.

As we worked together, I saw a different side of Emily-a side that was scared but still determined, a side that refused to let her past dictate her future. Her bravery in the face of adversity only made me more determined to protect her, to help her find a way out of this nightmare.

One night, as we wrapped up another long day of investigation, I couldn't help but feel a surge of admiration for her. Despite the fear and uncertainty, she never lost hope. She was fighting for her life, and I was fighting alongside her, every step of the way.

"You're doing great," I told her one evening as we took a break. "I know it's tough, but you're handling this better than anyone could expect. We'll get through this, Emily."

She gave me a tired smile, her eyes reflecting the exhaustion and determination that had become a part of our daily lives. "Thank you for being here," she said softly. "I know it's not easy, and I appreciate everything you're doing."

I nodded, feeling a deep sense of purpose. "It's my job to keep you safe," I said. "But it's also my choice. I care about you, Emily, and I'm not going anywhere."

The road ahead was fraught with challenges, but knowing that Emily and I were facing it together gave me hope. We were building something strong and resilient, a bond that was tested by adversity but strengthened by our shared determination to overcome it. And as we continued to navigate the dangers that lay ahead, I knew that we would emerge stronger, not just as individuals, but as a team.

Chapter 25

Emily's POV

The storm had passed, and with its departure came a semblance of peace. As the days turned into weeks, I found myself standing at a crossroads, the past and future stretching out before me like two divergent paths. The challenges we'd faced had left their mark, but they had also given me clarity.

Ryan and I had spent a lot of time talking, processing everything that had happened. He had been my rock, guiding me through the tumultuous waters of my past and helping me rediscover a sense of normalcy. Through it all, his presence had become a constant, a source of strength and comfort.

One crisp morning, as I stood by my motorcycle-now restored to its rightful place with a new license plate-Ryan joined me. He looked at me with a mix of curiosity and encouragement, sensing the shift in my demeanor.

"Ready to talk about it?" he asked, his voice gentle but inquisitive.

I took a deep breath, the fresh air filling my lungs and clearing my mind. "Yeah. I've been thinking a lot about what comes next. About finding a balance between who I was and who I want to be."

Ryan nodded, his gaze steady. "And what did you decide?"

"I want to ride again," I said, my voice firm with conviction. "But this time, responsibly. I need to honor Jake's memory in a way that reflects who I am now. I don't want to lose myself in the reckless persona I created. I want to ride with purpose."

His face lit up with a proud smile. "That sounds like a great plan. And I'll be right here with you, every step of the way."

Ryan's POV

Watching Emily come to this decision was nothing short of inspiring. Her journey had been fraught with pain and uncertainty, but seeing her stand tall and embrace a future that balanced both her love for riding and her desire for safety was a testament to her strength.

We spent the following weeks preparing for this new chapter. Emily took riding courses to refine her skills, ensuring that she was not only safe but also in control. We spent time together on the road, exploring new routes and rediscovering the joy of riding-this time, with a renewed sense of responsibility.

One weekend, as we rode through the winding roads of a picturesque countryside, Emily glanced over at me with a smile that was both genuine and content.

"This feels good," she said, her voice carrying over the wind. "It's like I'm finding my way back to who I was meant to be."

I reached out and touched her hand, my heart swelling with affection. "I'm glad to hear that. And I'm here with you, through all of it."

We found ourselves discussing our future more often now, our conversations filled with possibilities. We talked about opening a motorcycle shop, just as Emily and Jake had dreamed. It would be a place where people could come for repairs and advice, a place to share their passion for riding safely and responsibly. The idea excited us both, and it became a symbol of the new beginning we were forging together.

Emily's POV

The thought of opening the shop was exhilarating. It felt like a way to channel my grief and love for Jake into something positive, something that could help others. We began planning, working on business ideas and finding the perfect location. It was a project that gave me purpose and allowed me to honor Jake's memory in a way that felt right.

One evening, as Ryan and I sat in our small apartment surrounded by plans and sketches, he turned to me with a thoughtful expression.

"You know, we're building something really special here," he said. "It's not just about the shop. It's about our journey, the way we've grown together. I think we're creating something that's going to make a difference."

I looked at him, my heart full. "I couldn't have done any of this without you. Your support has meant everything to me."

He reached across the table and took my hand, his touch warm and reassuring. "And I couldn't have asked for a better partner in this journey. We've both been through so much, and now we're turning that into something meaningful."

As we continued to plan and dream about our future, I felt a renewed sense of hope and excitement. The road ahead was still uncertain, but it was one that we would navigate together. The challenges we had faced had brought us closer, and our shared vision for the future was a testament to our commitment to each other and to honoring Jake's memory.

Ryan's POV

Seeing Emily embrace this new beginning was profoundly moving. Her resilience and determination had turned what could have been a life marred by tragedy into a story of renewal and hope. Our shared dreams and plans were more than just ideas; they were symbols of our journey together and our commitment to creating a meaningful future.

As we rode together, our conversations about the shop and our life plans filled me with anticipation. I was eager to see where this new path would lead us, knowing that whatever challenges lay ahead, we would face them together.

Emily's decision to ride responsibly and pursue our shared dreams was a testament to her strength and to the love we had for each other. It was a reminder that even in the darkest moments, there is always a chance for a new beginning.

The road ahead was full of possibilities, and I was excited to see where it would take us. With Emily by my side and our dreams guiding us, I knew that the future was bright. And as we continued to build our life together, I was filled with a deep sense of gratitude and hope for what was to come.

Epilogue

Emily's POV

As Ryan and I embarked on this new chapter, our relationship continued to evolve. The journey was filled with moments of joy, discovery, and personal growth. Each day seemed like a new adventure, both in our lives and on the road. We learned more about each other with every mile we traveled and every challenge we faced.

One Saturday morning, we set out for a long ride through the mountains, our destination a secluded lake we had heard about from fellow bikers. The crisp, cool air and the rhythmic hum of the engine were soothing. We rode in comfortable silence, each of us lost in our thoughts.

When we reached the lake, it was even more beautiful than we had imagined. The water was a deep blue, surrounded by lush greenery. We unpacked a picnic and sat by the shore, enjoying the serenity.

"This place is perfect," Ryan said, spreading out the blanket. "It's moments like these that remind me why I fell for you."

I smiled, looking out at the tranquil water. "It's not just the adventures. It's the way you've been here for me, through everything. You've helped me heal and rediscover myself."

Ryan took my hand, his gaze steady. "And I wouldn't trade it for anything. You've brought so much into my life, and I'm grateful for every moment we share."

Ryan's POV

Our relationship continued to deepen as we navigated the complexities of life and love. Emily's transformation from The Ghost to someone who embraced both her past and her future was nothing short of extraordinary. We faced new challenges together, from managing the motorcycle shop to addressing lingering issues from Emily's past.

One evening, while we were working late at the shop, Emily's phone buzzed. She glanced at it, her expression darkening.

"Everything okay?" I asked, sensing her distress.

"It's an old contact from Jake's past," she replied, her voice tight. "They're asking questions about the shop and about me."

I reached out, placing a comforting hand on her shoulder. "We'll handle this together. Let's make sure we're prepared for any potential issues."

Emily's POV

The shop became a symbol of our new life, a place where we could create a positive impact while honoring Jake's memory. We dedicated time to community events and motorcycle safety workshops, using the shop as a platform to promote responsible riding.

One day, as we were setting up for a safety workshop, Ryan turned to me with a thoughtful expression. "You know, I've been thinking. We've come so far since those early days. From the chaos of the past to building this future together."

I nodded, feeling a sense of pride. "It's amazing to think about how much has changed. We've built something meaningful from the pain and loss."

Ryan smiled, his eyes filled with affection. "And we've done it together. I'm proud of what we've accomplished and excited about what's to come."

Ryan's POV

As we continued to build our life together, the challenges from the past seemed to fade into the background. The support and love we had for each other provided a solid foundation as we faced new obstacles.

One night, we sat together on the porch, watching the stars. Emily rested her head on my shoulder, and I felt a deep sense of contentment.

"This feels like home," she said softly. "We've created something beautiful out of everything we've been through."

I kissed the top of her head, feeling a surge of love. "I wouldn't want to be anywhere else. This is our home, and we've made it together."

Emily's POV

The final resolution of The Ghost's legacy came when we decided to publicly share our story. We held a charity ride in Jake's honor, raising funds for a cause that supported families affected by motorcycle accidents. The event was a success, and it felt like a fitting tribute to Jake's memory.

As the sun set on the day of the charity ride, Ryan and I stood together, looking out at the crowd of riders who had come to support the cause.

"This is incredible," I said, my voice filled with emotion. "It's like Jake's legacy is continuing through this event."

Ryan squeezed my hand. "It is. And we're carrying it forward with love and purpose. We've turned something painful into something that helps others."

Ryan's POV

Seeing Emily's growth and the positive impact we had made was deeply fulfilling. Her journey from The Ghost to someone who embraced life fully and responsibly was inspiring. Our relationship had weathered many storms, and we had emerged stronger and more connected.

As we looked toward the future, I knew that our love and our shared goals would continue to guide us. We had faced our past, embraced the present, and built a future filled with hope and possibility.

Emily's POV

With the past finally put to rest and a bright future ahead, Ryan and I looked forward to the adventures that awaited us. Our love had grown deeper, our bond stronger, and our dreams clearer. Together, we had found a new beginning, one that honored the past and embraced the promise of the future.

And as we rode into the sunset, side by side, I knew that no matter what challenges lay ahead, we would face them together-with love, strength, and a renewed sense of purpose.